Nancy Drew®
in
The Message in the Hollow Oak

*Nancy Drew Mystery Stories*® *in Armada*

* *For contractual reasons, Armada has been obliged to publish from No. 51 onwards before publishing Nos. 47–50. These missing numbers will be published as soon as possible.*

Nancy Drew Mystery Stories®

# The Message in the Hollow Oak

Carolyn Keene

**Armada**

First published in the U.K. in 1972 by
William Collins Sons & Co. Ltd, London and Glasgow
First published in Armada in 1973
This impression 1989

Armada is an imprint of
the Children's Division, part of
the Collins Publishing Group,
8 Grafton Street, London W1X 3LA

Printed and bound in Great Britain by
William Collins Sons & Co. Ltd, Glasgow

# CONTENTS

## A Winning Title

Carson Drew, Lawyer . . . Private.

Nancy frowned as she regarded the neatly-lettered sign on the door of her father's inner office. Her pretty face was flushed, and her blue eyes sparkled with excitement. She had such wonderful news to relate, yet it seemed that the door would never open. Conferences took entirely too long!

"It's hard to wait," she told Mr Drew's efficient secretary.

"I'd tell your father you are here, but he especially asked me not to disturb him."

"Oh, I don't want to interrupt him," Nancy said hastily. "I imagine the conference is very important, or it wouldn't take so long."

"Your father is conferring with Marcus Taylor."

Nancy looked up with interest.

"Not the builder who holds such extensive lumber interests in the north?"

"Yes, I believe that is the man. At any rate, I know Mr Taylor is bringing suit against a Canadian company, for I worked on the papers this morning."

"I've heard a great deal about him," Nancy remarked. "I should like to meet him very much."

She lowered her voice just then, for the inside office

7

door had opened. Carson Drew and a ruddy-cheeked man of about fifty emerged. The latter wore loose-fitting garments, and walked with the easy glide of one who has spent the greater part of his life out of doors.

"Well, Nancy, this is indeed a pleasant surprise," the lawyer smiled at his daughter, turning to present his companion to her. "Nancy, this is Mr Taylor."

"Chip off the old block, I'll warrant," the lumberman chuckled. "I've heard it said she could run you out of business, Mr Drew, if she was of a mind to!"

Nancy laughed at the compliment, and then changed the subject.

"I am taking a holiday from mysteries just now, Mr Taylor. I'm interested in television at present."

"Television?" her father inquired.

"Oh, Dad, that's what I came here to tell you!" Nancy could not withhold her news another instant. "I've won first prize in a TV contest!"

"I didn't even know that you had entered one," Carson Drew returned in surprise.

"I did it a short while ago on the spur of the moment, and then forgot all about it until the letter came today. You see, the Velvet Company offered a prize to the person who suggested the best mystery title for a serial written by Ann Chapelle. I watched each episode because the tale was so interesting. Just for the fun of it I sent in a title, never expecting to win. I was astonished when the letter and deed arrived."

"Deed?" her father inquired alertly.

"Yes. The Velvet Company also sent me a map so that I might find the land."

"Do you mean to tell me you've been awarded a piece of land, Nancy?"

"Yes, and I'm so excited about it. I've never owned land before."

"Where is this property?" her father demanded suspiciously. "Somewhere down in Florida, buried two feet under water?"

Nancy took the deed from her pocket and thrust it into Mr Drew's hand.

"Don't look so glum, Father," she said. "It's in Canada, and I'm sure it must be worth something."

"Worth the taxes on it," Carson Drew responded dryly. He glanced briefly at the paper, then handed it over to his companion. "You're familiar with Canadian land, Mr Taylor. Can you tell us anything about this place?"

"The property seems to be near Lake Wellington," the lumberman presently informed them. "I frequently spend my summers there."

"Then is it a nice place?" Nancy asked.

"Very pleasant in summer, but cold as Greenland in winter. The land is undeveloped, valued principally for its timber and mineral rights. But if it should be located near the lake, it might be used as a summer resort or a fishing camp."

"I fear it won't be worth anything," Nancy admitted, a trifle crestfallen.

"The best way to find out is to go there," Carson Drew declared cheerfully.

"There won't be much chance of that, from what Mr Taylor says. It's too far away," she sighed.

"It isn't that far away," Marcus Taylor smiled. "Wild country, of course, but not a great distance from a railroad."

"Why not go up there and look it over?" Mr Drew suggested.

Nancy stared in amazed delight.

"Do you really mean that, Dad?"

"Yes, if you can find someone responsible to accompany you. I'll be out of town for a week or so on business. That would be an excellent time for you to make the trip."

"Mr Taylor, you're not going to Lake Wellington, are you?" Nancy asked eagerly.

The lumberman shook his head regretfully.

"I wish I could get away for a few weeks, I'm so homesick for the smell of pine air. Can't make it, though, until my lawsuit is wiped off the slate. But I know a woman who is leaving for there in a few days!"

"Would she take me with her, do you think?" Nancy asked hopefully.

"She would if I were to ask her. We're old friends. Why, Mrs Taylor and I have stayed at Mrs Donnelly's boarding house every summer we've spent in the north. She's a motherly soul and would take good care of you."

"Where is she now?" Carson Drew questioned.

"She's expected in River Heights within a few days, I understand. She has been visiting a sister living nearby, but is coming on here. She'll be returning to Canada shortly to open up her boarding house for the summer."

"May I go with her, Dad?" Nancy asked.

"If she's willing to take you along, I see no reason why you shouldn't make the trip. I'll speak to her at the very first opportunity."

"I wish Bess and George could go with me, too," Nancy went on, thinking aloud. "What a lark that would be!"

Few persons guessed that George Fayne and Bess Marvin were girl cousins, so unlike were they in appearance. Bess was blonde and a little plump while George had short dark hair and a slim athletic figure.

"What would you think of Mrs Donnelly chaperoning the girls and myself?" Nancy asked her father.

"I'd feel sorry for the poor woman!" he teased. "But all joking aside, I think it's splendid that you have won the land, and I hope it turns out to be valuable."

Nancy took leave of the lumberman and her father. Then, with the precious deed in her bag, she hurried away to show it to her friends, George and Bess.

She tripped along with a light step, so engrossed in daydreaming that she hardly noticed where she was going. The loud toot of a car horn sounded in her ears. Looking round, she realized that she was at the busy street crossing opposite the National Bank.

As she waited for the signal to cross the street she saw an elderly lady coming towards her, bent low beneath the weight of a heavy suitcase. Impulsively Nancy rushed to the stranger's aid.

"You shouldn't carry such a big load," the girl chided gently. "Please let me help you."

With a tired sigh the white-haired woman relinquished her burden.

"I am almost worn out," she admitted, smiling at Nancy. "You see, I expected a man to meet me here but he failed to keep the appointment. Maybe you've seen him—he'd be in a dark red car."

Nancy shook her head.

"I haven't, but he may be along any minute. Have you far to go?"

"Several blocks," she replied. "However, I must stop at a bank to change a note."

"The National Bank is just across the street," Nancy

indicated. "If you like, I'll stay here with the suitcase while you do your errand."

"That's very kind of you, I'm sure. It will take me only five minutes."

The woman cautiously made her way across the street, and disappeared into the bank. Ten minutes later a dark red car drew up to the kerb. The driver, a dapper man in his late thirties, hailed Nancy.

"I'll take that suitcase, young lady," he cried.

Nancy regarded him suspiciously.

"I am keeping it for an elderly lady."

"Sure, I know," he smiled disarmingly. "She's my grandmother."

"Then you're the man in the red car who was supposed to meet her?"

"That's right. I was held up in a traffic jam."

The man got out of the car, and before Nancy could protest took the suitcase and placed it in the boot.

"I'll run over to the bank and tell her you're waiting," Nancy offered.

She hurried across the street. Entering the building, she was greatly relieved to meet the elderly woman just inside the doorway.

"Your grandson is waiting for you," Nancy explained. "He drove up in the car and I left the suitcase with him."

"But I have no grandson."

Nancy was bewildered.

"This man drove up in a dark red car, and said you were his grandmother. I hope I haven't made a mistake——"

In a panic she rushed out to the street. Her worst fears were confirmed. The man and the red car had vanished!

# ·2·

## *The Theft*

"HE'S gone!"

Nancy's heart sank as she realized how easily she had been fooled.

"Oh, it was all my fault," she declared self-accusingly. "Was the case very valuable?"

"Yes, it contained some papers which I can't afford to lose," the woman returned, trying to hide her distress. "Perhaps the suitcase hasn't been stolen after all. The driver may actually have been my friend."

Nancy quickly described the stranger's appearance.

"He was of early middle age and well dressed, though somewhat flashily so. His hair was fair, his eyes sharp and piercing."

"Then it couldn't have been the one who was to meet me, for his hair is dark. Oh, I'm afraid you are right. The case has been stolen. What shall I do?"

"We must notify the police."

Nancy had glimpsed a policeman at the next corner, and hurriedly told him the details of the theft. He glanced sharply at Nancy and questioned her companion further.

"Where did you meet this girl? Did you mention to her that the bag contained valuables?"

"I met her on the street, and she offered to help me

carry the suitcase. I don't believe I told her it was valuable until after it had disappeared."

"If you have any doubts about me you can ask almost anyone here in River Heights," Nancy said proudly. "My father, Carson Drew, is well known in the city."

"You're Carson Drew's daughter?" the policeman exclaimed.

"Yes, I am."

"Then I'll vouch for her honesty, Ma'am."

"I am Mrs Donnelly from Canada," the woman informed the policeman. "I never doubted this young lady's honesty, for I pride myself upon being a good judge of character. The man in the red car stole the case."

Nancy was amazed when she learned the identity of the woman whom she had befriended, though she did not at that moment comment on the coincidence.

"Did you take the number of the car?" the policeman asked her.

Nancy was forced to admit that she had not. However, she gave a detailed description of the man as well as his car.

"I'll phone headquarters right away," the policeman promised. "The patrol car may be able to pick him up."

"I'm afraid the case has gone," Mrs Donnelly said disconsolately, after the policeman had left to telephone. "I don't know what I shall do unless I get it back, for it contains my return ticket to Canada."

Nancy made a sudden decision.

"My car is parked only a block from here. I'll get it and chase the thief myself!"

Mrs Donnelly clutched the girl's arm nervously.

"Oh no, you mustn't do that! It would be too dangerous!"

"I'll take no unnecessary risks. That man has a good start, and if we wait until his description has been broadcast by the police it may be too late for us to overtake him."

"Then see if you can trace the car," Mrs Donnelly urged gratefully, "but be careful. I'll wait in the bank until you return."

Nancy ran to the car, and a moment later had it in motion. She was not very confident that she could catch the red car, yet it seemed reasonable to her to believe that the thief would take the main street which led to the outskirts of River Heights.

Luck had always favoured Nancy; she also had considerable resourcefulness and courage, and her interest in mysteries had earned her an enviable reputation as a detective. Her father, a noted criminal lawyer, was very proud of her ability, and enjoyed discussing unusual aspects of his work with her.

Bess and George, who lived near each other, usually shared in Nancy's adventures. Nothing piqued the cousins more than to be excluded from a mystery.

"I wonder what they'll say when I tell them about my meeting Mrs Donnelly under such odd circumstances," Nancy reflected, skilfully guiding her car through heavy traffic. "Unless I can manage to overtake that thief, I'll feel a little ashamed to tell the story."

As she reached the less congested part of the city, Nancy gained speed, driving a little faster than the law allowed.

"If I'm arrested, I'll have a good reason for it, at least," she told herself.

Then, as she was approaching traffic lights, she slowed down. The lights changed to green just as Nancy came to a standstill and at that instant she caught a glimpse of a red car crossing the intersection!

Nancy accelerated the engine and began the pursuit. Taking the driver of the other car by surprise, she succeeded in drawing abreast. One glance told her that the driver was the man who had stolen the suitcase!

As she tooted her horn, the culprit gave her a panic-stricken look, and speeded up, but Nancy did not intend to be outdistanced. Again she overtook the car.

"Stop!" she cried out.

The man paid no attention, so Nancy tooted her horn to attract the attention of passing motorists. Suddenly, with a sharp twist of the driving wheel she crossed directly in front of the red car, blocking its path. The thief would have to stop or else cause a crash.

For one terrifying moment Nancy thought he intended to keep on. But suddenly, to the sound of screeching brakes, his car came to a quivering halt. The man sprang out and started to run.

"Stop him!" Nancy cried out. "Don't let him escape!"

By this time a number of cars had halted, and pedestrians were gathering. Two men overtook the thief, dragging him back to the car.

"He stole an old lady's suitcase," Nancy cried. "The police are after him."

"It's a lie," the man snarled, struggling to free himself.

Nancy ran to the back of the red car, raising the lid of the boot. Triumphantly she displayed Mrs Donnelly's case.

*The red car was forced to screech to a halt . . .*

"That's mine," the thief insisted angrily. "This silly girl has mistaken me for someone else."

However, the crowd seemed inclined to believe Nancy's story and the two men held the thief firmly until he was turned over to police officers.

"If you are innocent it will be an easy matter for you to prove it at headquarters," Nancy assured the prisoner as he was taken away. "The suitcase will be opened there in the presence of Mrs Donnelly."

"You'll pay for this outrage!" the man snapped.

Nancy followed the police in her own car, pausing only long enough to pick up Mrs Donnelly, who was waiting in the National Bank.

"Goodness me, I don't see how you managed to overtake that man so quickly," the elderly lady praised Nancy. "I never expected to see the case again. "

At the police station Mrs Donnelly promptly identified her suitcase, then confronted the prisoner. She stiffened slightly as she saw him.

"Tom Stripe!" she cried. "I've always known you were mean and low-down, but I never thought you'd stoop to become a common thief!"

"You know this man!" Nancy asked in amazement.

"Know him? Of course I do. He made trouble between another family and my own. Of late he's held a grudge against me because of a valuable piece of timberland I have near Wellington Lake."

"We'll see that he doesn't bother you for some time at least," an officer promised. "A few weeks in jail will do him good."

"I wish you would accept a reward for recovering my suitcase," the Canadian woman urged Nancy as the two left the police station together.

"Oh, I couldn't do that. I'm as relieved as you are to get the case again because I felt responsible for its loss. If you'll tell me where you are staying, I'll take you there in my car."

Mrs Donnelly hesitated a moment.

"I wrote to some friends that I was coming. I am not certain now that they are expecting me, as they did not meet me."

"I'll be glad to take you wherever you wish to go."

"Then I think I'll go to the Taylor house, anyway. Marcus Taylor and his wife are old friends of mine. I've known Marcus nearly thirty years—ever since he was a lumberjack."

"I met Mr Taylor for the first time today," Nancy said. "For years the old house has been closed, so the family isn't very well known in River Heights."

"Marcus spends most of his time in the north. He's a fine man and a loyal friend."

"He spoke very highly of you."

Mrs Donnelly looked surprised as well as pleased.

"Did he say anything about expecting me to visit here?"

"Why, I believe he said you intended to visit your sister, and come to River Heights later."

"That's what I wrote in my first letter. Later I received word from my sister that she wouldn't be at home for several days, so I wrote to Marcus again, asking if his son would meet me. I hope he got the letter."

"No doubt he did. I shouldn't worry about it. I know where the Taylors live so I'll drive you there."

A few minutes later Nancy parked her car in front of the rambling, old-fashioned house. She carried the heavy suitcase up the path and set it down on the porch. Anxiously Mrs Donnelly rang the bell.

"I do hope they're at home," she said nervously.

Marcus Taylor appeared at the door. From the expression on his face it was obvious that he was not looking for Mrs Donnelly. Nevertheless, he greeted her heartily and insisted that Nancy also come in for a few minutes.

"I can tell you weren't looking for me," Mrs Donnelly declared uneasily. "Didn't you get the letter I sent from Chicago?"

"It must have got lost," Marcus Taylor returned, "but that doesn't make any difference. We always have an extra room for you. I've been wanting to see you today anyway, because I have a favour to ask of you."

"What is it?" Mrs Donnelly smiled.

Marcus Taylor winked at Nancy.

"When you return to Wellington Lake, I want you to chaperon a young lady friend of mine."

"I'll be glad to do that, Marcus, but I hope she isn't one of these silly modern creatures who can't do a thing for themselves."

"You should be a judge of that because you've already met her!"

Mrs Donnelly stared at Nancy.

"Surely he doesn't mean you!" she gasped.

"I'm afraid he does," Nancy laughed. "Our meeting was a strange coincidence."

"A fortunate one for me, my dear. I'll be glad to take you back with me to Wellington Lake. But tell me, what takes you to such an isolated spot?"

Nancy explained about the contest, and impulsively offered the deed for Mrs Donnelly's inspection. To the girl's satisfaction, the woman put on her spectacles and studied the paper carefully.

"Well, what do you think of it?" Marcus Taylor demanded, as she finally returned the document to Nancy. "You're a clever trader when it comes to a land deal, Mrs Donnelly. If you say the property is valueless it might save the girl a hard trip."

Mrs Donnelly hesitated a long while before offering her opinion.

"I don't like to build up false hopes for one really can't be sure of a thing."

"I wish you would give me your honest opinion," Nancy urged. "After all, the land cost me nothing, so if it should prove to be worthless I won't have suffered."

"I think the property would merit investigating," Mrs Donnelly declared firmly. "In fact, it may prove to be more valuable than anyone expects."

"Meaning what?" the lumberman demanded.

"Meaning that this land is located in a section where gold has been discovered! Few people know of it yet, for the secret has been carefully guarded. I shouldn't disclose it, only Miss Drew befriended me today, and I always like to repay favours."

Marcus Taylor whistled softly.

"Nancy Drew, it looks to me as if you really won a prize when you selected that lucky TV title. If it should turn out that there's gold on your land, you may make a fortune!"

A faraway look had come over Nancy's face. Her eyes grew brilliant.

"Gold," she said half to herself. "That settles it! Now I know I'm going to Wellington Lake, and we can't start too soon to suit me!"

# ·3·

## An Eventful Journey

IN GLANCING through the mail the following morning,
Nancy was pleasantly surprised to find a brief note from
Mrs Taylor, inviting Carson Drew and herself to have
dinner at their house that evening.

"How nice of her to ask us!" she exclaimed in delight.
"You'll be able to go, won't you, Dad?"

"I think I can make it," the lawyer said. "It will give
me a chance to talk to Mrs Donnelly about your trip."

"I'm looking forward to it," Nancy replied. "If what
she says is true about gold——"

"I'd not put much stock in that story, Nancy. It's not
likely that a company would give away such a valuable
piece of land."

"Not if they suspected it to be extremely valuable, of
course. I suppose it is foolish of me to hope, yet I can't
help but feel lucky about this property. What's more, if
Bess and George go with me, I know I'll have an
exciting trip."

Nancy had told her friends about the proposed trip
the previous day. Both girls were very eager to go, and
now when Nancy called at the Marvin house shortly
after breakfast, she found them there discussing the
prospects.

"All aboard for Lake Wellington!" George greeted her gaily.

"Will you both really be able to go?" Nancy questioned eagerly.

"I think so. Our mothers have practically consented."

The girls fell to discussing various details of the proposed trip, including the clothes they were to take. Bess was inclined to want to pack her best dresses, but Nancy discouraged her, pointing out that they would need sturdy shoes and tough, warm garments in the woods. Presently she glanced at the clock, and was startled to see how quickly time had passed.

"I must hurry home," she announced, rising. "I promised Hannah I'd bake a chocolate cake for lunch."

She found kindly Mrs Gruen, the warm-hearted housekeeper, busy in the spick-and-span white kitchen. Hannah Gruen had lived with Nancy and her father since the death of Mrs Drew when Nancy was three years old.

"I thought you wouldn't be here, Nancy," she remarked, as the girl donned an apron. "I'd have stirred up the cake myself, only the ones I make never come out as well as yours do."

"Flatterer!" Nancy laughed. "It was you who taught me how to bake chocolate cake."

"So I did, but the pupil has gone beyond the master. Oh, by the way, there was a telephone call for you this morning."

"From one of the girls?"

"No, it was from a man. He wouldn't give me his name."

"That's strange. It was probably a salesman," Nancy said, immediately forgetting about the mysterious call as she busied herself with the cake.

Promptly at seven that evening the Drews presented themselves at the Taylor house, where they were warmly welcomed. Nancy was delighted to observe that her father and Mrs Donnelly took an instant liking to each other. During dinner the conversation centred on his daughter's newly-acquired property.

"I shouldn't mind owning that property myself," Mrs Donnelly smiled warmly at Nancy. "It may turn out to be worthless, yet in my opinion it presents a wonderful speculation. If there should be gold——"

She did not finish the sentence, for at that moment a maid entered the room to say that Nancy was wanted on the telephone. Excusing herself, she went to answer the call and was away for several minutes. When she returned everyone noticed the strange expression on her face.

"Father, did you ever hear of a man named Raymond Niles?" she asked quickly, as she resumed her place at the table.

The lawyer shook his head.

"It's strange," Nancy went on. "He wanted to buy my land."

"How much did he offer you for it?" Mr Drew questioned.

"A hundred dollars."

"He must be a swindler!" Mrs Donnelly announced, before the lawyer could offer a similar opinion. "If the land is worth anything it's worth far more than that."

"That's what I thought," Nancy said quietly. "I told him my ground wasn't for sale."

"Did that satisfy him?" her father asked.

"No. Then he asked to see my deed. He was very persistent."

"I'd have nothing whatever to do with him, Nancy."

"I don't intend to. I made him understand that I would not show the paper to anyone. I probably won't hear from him again."

But the following afternoon as Nancy was walking slowly towards the public library, a handsome young man with curly blond hair and a sophisticated smile accosted her at a street corner.

"Miss Drew, I believe?"

"Yes," she assented, trying not to stare at the youth's clothes, which were in the height of fashion and looked out of place in River Heights.

"I am Raymond Niles," he declared disarmingly.

Nancy stiffened.

"I am sorry, Mr Niles, but I do not care to sell my property to you."

"Oh, I understand that, Miss Drew. But it adjoins some land which a friend of mine owns in Canada, and for a certain legal reason I should like to examine the deed."

"I cannot show it to you," Nancy returned, growing annoyed. "Please let me pass."

Instead of standing aside, the man fell in step with her.

"I would pay you a small consideration——"

"As far as I am concerned, the subject is no longer of interest, Mr Niles! If you don't stop annoying me I shall call a policeman!"

"All right, if that's the way you feel about it." Abruptly the young man turned away. "But you'll be sorry you didn't deal with me!"

Nancy was disturbed by the incident, and reported the encounter to her father.

"I could notify the police," he told her thoughtfully, "but that would advertise the fact that your land may be valuable. It seems to me we ought to let the matter rest for a while. In any event, you will be rid of this fellow in a few days, for soon you'll be on your way to Canada."

Mr Drew had completed all the arrangements with Mrs Donnelly for the Canadian woman to chaperon Nancy, Bess and George to Wellington Lake and the girls were so excited they could hardly wait.

Then two days before the scheduled departure, Raymond Niles telephoned the Drew home.

"You haven't changed your mind about that deed?" he inquired a trifle insolently.

"No, Mr Niles!" Nancy retorted and she hung up before he could continue the conversation.

The precious document was in the top drawer of a desk in Mr Drew's study. Nancy would have felt better about it if it had been placed in a less obvious hideaway. However, it seemed foolish to go to the trouble of taking it to the bank for such a brief period, since she intended to take it with her on her journey north.

Time was growing short, and Nancy was too busy packing to give much thought to Raymond Niles, although once Bess had seen him lurking near the Drew house. A dozen times a day the cousins would run over to the house to chat excitedly about the trip or to seek advice concerning their wardrobes.

"Everything is ready," Nancy informed Hannah as she finished strapping the last bag. "Our train leaves at seven tonight, and I'm going to the bank now for some money. I'll be back in half an hour."

She was away from the house longer than she had

anticipated, and on her return just after four o'clock, she entered the kitchen to find it deserted.

"Hannah!" she called.

"Coming," the housekeeper replied from the general direction of the study. An instant later the woman bustled into the room.

"Oh, Nancy, I'm so glad you've returned," she began anxiously, "for I didn't know what to do when that man came for the paper you promised him."

"What paper?" the girl asked quickly.

"A deed you keep in the desk drawer. This chap was mighty handsome and said he was a good friend of yours."

"You didn't give the paper to him?" Nancy demanded in alarm.

"Yes, I did, but he's still in the library, for I told him to wait there. Oh, I hope I haven't done anything wrong!"

Nancy darted towards the study. As she had feared, it was empty. Raymond Niles had tricked Hannah!

Panic-stricken at the thought of losing the valuable paper, Nancy raced towards the front door. She caught a glimpse of the man moving hurriedly across the porch.

"Wait!" she called sharply.

As he wheeled round, the girl sprang forward and caught him by the arm.

"Give me my deed!" she cried.

The man tried to thrust the document into his pocket, but Nancy snatched it from him.

"You are a thief!" she accused him. "Leave this house at once, or I'll turn you over to the police!"

Raymond Niles muttered something Nancy could not catch. She closed the door in his face.

"I thought he was a friend of yours, or I'd never have trusted him," Hannah said in distress.

"Don't worry about it now," the girl returned kindly. "It wasn't your fault. Anyway, I saved it, and that's all that matters."

The few remaining hours before train time passed all too swiftly. At the station Hannah was quite tearful as she bade her young mistress farewell.

"I won't rest a minute until you're safely back in River Heights," she declared.

Nancy glanced uneasily about the busy station platform, but could not see her father. She wondered what could be keeping him. He had telephoned her at the house, telling her he would meet her at the station, but the signal now warned her the train was approaching, and still Mr Drew had not appeared.

"What can be delaying Dad?" she fretted. "I can't start off without saying goodbye to him."

At that instant Bess caught sight of the lawyer driving up in a taxi. Nancy rushed over to greet him.

"Nancy," he said hurriedly, "several things have happened since I saw you last. I'm not sure but I think it's a mistake to allow you to make this trip——"

"Oh, Dad——"

"I'll not change my mind about it now, but I must warn you to be very careful. I'm a trifle uneasy about this land of yours."

"I don't understand."

"There's something going on that I don't exactly like." Carson Drew spoke hurriedly, for the train was almost in. "I've just learned that Tom Stripe is out of jail on bail."

"But what has that to do with my land?"

"Perhaps nothing. However, bail was provided by Raymond Niles."

"Indicating that they are friends and crooks."

"Undoubtedly. Now, it may mean nothing at all, but while you're at Wellington Lake be very careful."

"I will be," Nancy promised seriously.

Carson Drew bent down to kiss his daughter goodbye as the train came thundering into the station. A moment later Nancy stepped aboard, and with Mrs Donnelly and her friends she began the long journey to Wellington Lake.

Mrs Donnelly ordered her berth to be made up shortly after she boarded the train. The girls were far too excited to sleep, however. They wandered into the observation coach where they interested themselves with various magazines and newspapers.

Soon Nancy became absorbed in a fascinating story entitled *The Vital Hour*, but casually glanced up from her reading as a distinguished-looking woman of about thirty-five entered the coach and took a seat nearby.

"I see you are reading one of my stories," the newcomer presently remarked.

Nancy looked up with interest.

"Then your name is——"

"That particular story is published under a pseudonym. As a rule I use my own name, Ann Chapelle."

Nancy stared.

"You're not Ann Chapelle who wrote the serial for the Velvet Hour?"

"Yes, I am," the other smiled.

"Why, I followed them all! If it hadn't been for you, I shouldn't be on this train now. You see, I won the title contest and am on my way to Wellington Lake,

Canada, to look over the piece of land which was the prize."

It was Miss Chapelle's turn to be astonished.

"Then you must be Nancy Drew! I knew your title had been selected, but I never dreamed I'd ever meet you in person."

"Do you expect to write another play soon?" Nancy inquired hopefully.

"Not for some time, I imagine. I am now busy with a novel, and my film contracts keep me busy."

"You must know many famous film stars."

"I do," Miss Chapelle acknowledged. "However, I must confess I attend few parties. I don't care a great deal for them."

The woman lapsed into a moody silence which Nancy hesitated to interrupt. Despite her interesting life, the young writer seemed to be unhappy.

Nancy was on the point of asking a question when there was suddenly a shrill whistle from the train engine, followed by a terrific crash. Nancy was flung headlong from her seat. Splintered boards, battered furniture and debris descended on her.

For a moment the girl was too stunned to move. Then, as she squirmed to a sitting position she felt a sharp pain in her arm. Carefully she moved it, relieved to discover that it had not been broken. A trickle of blood oozed from a cut in her forehead.

All about her Nancy could hear people groaning. She staggered to her feet, looking about her for Bess and George. She found George half hidden under a pile of chairs.

"I'll get you out in a minute," Nancy encouraged. A moment later she had helped the stunned girl up.

"What happened?" George murmured.

"There's been a crash. Are you hurt?"

"Only shaken up a bit, I think. Is Bess safe?"

"I haven't found her yet."

"She was sitting right beside me when the crash came."

Anxiously the girls began to move the debris, peering carefully beneath each pile. A low moan drew them to the place where their friend lay. Her face was so white they thought she must be seriously injured.

"Bess!" Nancy dropped to her knees.

"Where am I?" the victim mumbled.

Tenderly the girls lifted her and carried her to a level spot outside the coach. Nancy chafed her friend's hands and spread out her coat for her to lie on.

"Don't bother about me," Bess directed presently. "I'm dazed from a blow on the head, but I'll soon be all right. Help the others."

"Let's try to find Mrs Donnelly and Miss Chapelle," Nancy suggested.

Anxiously she and George looked about for the two women, but did not see them among the little group of uninjured. Returning to the observation coach, they helped a child who had been pinned under a steel beam, and lifted out a boy with a broken leg.

Almost every coach had left the tracks. Nancy noted that the coach which Mrs Donnelly had occupied had received the brunt of the impact, and some compartments were ablaze. The flames, whipped by a strong wind, were spreading rapidly.

"Get some helpers and see if you can find Miss Chapelle," Nancy called to George. "I'll make certain that Mrs Donnelly is safe."

Nancy grew bewildered as she tried to locate Mrs Donnelly. The coach she was in had been transformed into a tangled, twisted mass of steel. Flames were creeping closer and closer.

Over and over she called Mrs Donnelly's name, but there was no response. All about her women were crying hysterically, while children were sobbing and searching for their parents. Nancy felt physically ill, yet she continued pulling away debris, working desperately to beat the creeping line of red flame.

Just then George came running back to help her.

"Have you found Miss Chapelle?" Nancy asked.

"No. I've hunted everywhere. I'd have kept on looking, only I thought you might need me here."

"I do. Oh, George, I'm afraid we'll not get to her in time——"

At that moment a glad shout went up, for the rescue team had been sighted!

"Thank goodness, they've come at last!" Nancy exclaimed.

Even as she spoke, a burning brand, carried by the wind, dropped at her feet. She stamped it out, but still others fell about her.

In another minute the carriage would be on fire!

# ·4·

## Disaster

NANCY and George stood helplessly by, watching the rescue team at work.

In response to Nancy's frantic plea the rescue team had bravely battled the fire, removing several people from the flaming coach. Mrs Donnelly, however, had not been among those rescued.

"We may find her yet," one of the rescuers told Nancy, "but it looks bad."

"It's possible she was rescued before we got here," George said hopefully.

Nancy nodded, trying to keep up her spirits. She could not acknowledge to herself that Mrs Donnelly might be dead.

The night was very black, the only light being that provided by torches and lanterns brought along by the rescue team. Many of the injured passengers had been taken to hospitals and nearby houses. It was possible that in the confusion they had failed to see Mrs Donnelly. This hope gave them fresh courage.

"We may as well go back to Bess," Nancy proposed, "for we can do no good here."

The girls found Bess in much better condition than when they had left her. She was wrapped in a warm blanket to protect her from the cold night air.

"How is Mrs Donnelly?" she asked instantly.

"She hasn't been found yet," Nancy said quietly. "But we still have hope."

Bess was silent for a time: then she said soberly:

"This crash has been a terrible thing. I hate to think that anything has happened to Mrs Donnelly or to that new acquaintance of yours, Nancy."

"Miss Chapelle?"

"Yes. She hasn't been found, either."

"Almost everyone in the observation coach escaped lightly," Nancy said thoughtfully. "It's a mystery what became of her."

"A great many strange things have happened to-night," Bess declared significantly. "For instance, what could have caused the crash?"

"The men said it was an open switch," George told her.

"I suppose it was an accident, all right," Bess agreed, "but I grew suspicious when I saw Raymond Niles and another man in the throng here tonight!"

"Can you describe his companion?" Nancy questioned.

"Not very well, I'm afraid. He was about forty, I should say. A dapper sort of man, though not as well dressed as Niles."

Nancy remembered what her father had told her just as the train had pulled into the River Heights station. Raymond Niles had provided bail for Tom Stripe. Bess's description fitted the latter very well. Could it be possible that the two had boarded the train with the intention of following Nancy to Wellington Lake?

"I must be on my guard," she thought, "but I'll not worry Bess and George by telling them what I fear."

For nearly an hour the three girls stayed at the scene

of the crash. By then, Nancy's nerves had begun to give way under the strain, and her friends observed that she, too, had been injured.

"You must see a doctor immediately," Bess insisted.

"It's nothing," Nancy maintained. "I'll be quite all right after a night's rest. If we only knew what has become of Mrs Donnelly and Miss Chapelle!"

"You'll make yourself ill if you don't stop worrying," George advised her kindly. "I can't help feeling they are both safe."

"We should know the worst by morning," Nancy said quietly. "There is no point in our staying here. I suggest that we spend the rest of the night at a hotel."

The others readily agreed to the suggestion, for they were exhausted from their harrowing experience. A bus took them to the nearby town of Windham, close to the Canadian border, where they booked a room at the Hamilton Hotel.

Before going to bed, Nancy sent a telegram to her father, telling him that she was safe. Bess and George sent similar messages to their parents.

"I believe I'll not be able to sleep a wink," Bess declared nervously, as her friends tucked blankets about her. "I feel positively unnerved."

"So do I," Nancy acknowledged, "but we should be thankful we're alive and uninjured."

"And that our luggage wasn't destroyed," George added. "Nancy, did you manage to save your property papers?"

"Yes, they were in my bag, which I had all the time."

Nancy indicated the handbag which lay on the dresser. Bess regarded it fixedly, then closed her eyes and dropped off into a troubled sleep.

George, too, was so exhausted that she fell into a deep slumber almost as soon as her head touched the pillow. At first Nancy was so restless and worried that she could not sleep, though presently she dozed off.

She awoke when it was still dark and experienced a strange sensation. It seemed as though someone had called to her.

Sitting up, she looked about the hotel room. George was sleeping peacefully at her side. She looked towards the bed occupied by Bess, but it was empty.

Thoroughly alarmed, Nancy thrust aside the covers and sprang out of bed. She tried the door and found it still locked from the inside. Next she ran to the open window. A cry of horror escaped her as she gazed downwards.

Bess, apparently walking in her sleep, had climbed out on to the fire escape. Then she had descended until she was on a level with a window ledge. At the moment she stood teetering on the narrow slab of concrete! At any second she might plunge to her death!

Nancy's cry had disturbed George. "What is it?" she murmured drowsily.

"Don't make a sound," Nancy warned fearfully. "Come here."

George crept to the open window. At the sight below, she stifled an exclamation of fear.

"If we waken her she will be sure to fall," Nancy whispered, shuddering as she glanced down at the garden below. "I'm going to try to get to her."

It was a mystery how Bess had managed to climb over to the narrow ledge. She was poised far out of reach. Even from the fire escape Nancy could not follow without risking her own life.

"I'll have to try some other way," she decided, returning to the bedroom window.

"We can never rescue her on our own," George said. "I'll run downstairs for help."

She drew on a dressing gown, then disappeared.

Left to herself, Nancy watched Bess fearfully. The girl would be safe if she remained where she was, but at any moment she might take a step forward, which would send her hurtling down to the ground below.

Unable to endure the suspense of waiting for help, Nancy rushed to an upstairs corridor. Suddenly she saw a coiled rope left by a workman. Snatching it up, she ran to a window directly over the spot where Bess was standing.

A minute later George, followed by two frightened hotel porters, raced back into the vacant bedroom.

"There she is!" George cried, as she pointed to the ghostly white figure on the ledge.

Her words ended in a shrill scream. Bess's foot had slipped. The horrified observers saw her pitch forward in a plunge towards the garden!

# ·5·

## Lost and Found

At THAT very moment a rope swished through the air and settled neatly round Bess's shoulders. From the window above Nancy drew it tight and held the girl back against the ledge.

The near fall had wakened Bess. Suddenly aware of her situation, she uttered a terrified cry for help, and cringed against the wall.

"Don't move! We'll get you in a minute," Nancy called.

George and the two men had already gone out onto the fire escape. With Nancy helping from above by the skilful use of her rope, they managed to reach the frightened girl, and support her back to the bedroom. Bess slumped down in a little heap.

"I was never so frightened before in all my life! Nancy, if you hadn't thrown that rope when you did, I'd surely have been killed."

"That little trick I learned at Shadow Ranch is certainly useful. Fortunately, I didn't miss my aim."

After the two attendants had left, the girls plied Bess with questions.

"I have no more idea than you why I did it," Bess told them ruefully. "As far as I know, I have never walked in my sleep before. I suppose it was because I was so upset about the crash. And I had such an awful nightmare."

"What was it like?" George asked curiously.

"Oh, I can't remember the first part of it—but some dreadful animal seemed to be pursuing me. Then I thought someone was after Nancy's papers. Anyway, I thought I'd get up and put them in a safer place. I remember going over to the dresser. The next moment I woke up to find myself on that ledge." Bess shuddered again at the realization of what might have happened to her.

Nancy, reminded of the precious deed, glanced towards the dresser where she had left her bag. It had gone.

"Bess, you don't suppose you actually picked up the bag, do you?" she inquired anxiously. Just then she saw the bag lying open on the carpet, and snatched it up. One glance inside revealed that the deed was missing.

"Oh, what have I done!" Bess exclaimed in distress. "You don't suppose I actually took your papers and hid them somewhere, do you?"

"It begins to look as if you did," Nancy was forced to say ruefully.

George was struck by a sudden thought. "Bess had something white in her hand when we first saw her standing on that ledge! Perhaps she dropped the deed into the garden. I'll see if it's lying there now."

She crossed over to the window and peered out. Involuntarily she gave a cry of dismay.

"What is it?" Nancy cried, rushing to the window.

She caught a glimpse of a man retreating down an alley.

"I saw him pick up a paper from beneath the

window!" George announced tensely. "I was too startled to call out until he had moved away. Oh, Nancy, I'm just as sure as anything that it was your lost deed!"

"It's useless to go after him, for he's too far away now," Nancy said in a discouraged tone. "I suppose the paper is lost and with it my chances of ever claiming my Canadian property."

"It's all my fault," Bess accused herself gloomily. "If I had the money, I'd pay you for that land."

Nancy squeezed her chum's hand.

"Don't feel bad about it, Bess," she said thoughtfully. "There's a possibility the deed will be returned. At any rate, I'll put an ad in the paper tomorrow. The man who picked up the document may see it and apply for a reward."

Bess felt too upset over the entire matter to go back to sleep. Since it was almost five o'clock, the girls finished their dressing and sent downstairs for hot coffee. As soon as the dining room opened they had breakfast. Yet, despite Nancy's attempts to keep up a cheerful conversation, a feeling of deep gloom prevailed.

At their first opportunity the girls placed an advertisement in the local evening paper, offering a reward for the return of the missing deed. Scarcely had they finished telephoning, than the hotel clerk called them over to the desk.

"I have good news for you at last," he told the girls cheerfully.

"Our friends have been saved?" Bess gasped.

"Yes. Mrs Donnelly and Miss Chapelle are both at the Good Hope Hospital. The best thing for you to do will be to drive out there. It's about five miles away."

"We'll start just as soon as we can find a car," Nancy decided.

With the aid of the helpful clerk they found a driver to take them to the Good Hope Hospital. As they were leaving town Nancy caught a glimpse of the newspaper office.

"Stop here just a minute," she directed the driver, and explained to Bess and George, "I want to run in and see if my advertisement has been copied correctly."

She vanished into the building, to return in a few minutes, a letter clutched in her hand. Triumphantly she flashed it before George and Bess.

"It couldn't be an answer to your advertisement!" the latter gasped. "That would be impossible because the paper hasn't come out yet!"

"Shortly after I telephoned this morning, a man came into the office and left this letter. He told the editor to give it to anyone claiming to have lost an important paper near the Hamilton Hotel!"

"What does the note say?" George demanded impatiently.

Nancy ripped open the envelope and scanned the brief message. She looked slightly disappointed.

"Why, it doesn't say a thing about the lost deed. It just asks me to call at the Ranny farm six miles south of Windham. We must drive out there at the first opportunity. If it should happen that my deed has been recovered, I'll feel greatly relieved."

"If you get the paper back, we may be able to go on to Wellington Lake a little later," George added a trifle wistfully. "Just think—if everything hadn't gone wrong we'd be there now."

A brief ride over bumpy roads brought the girls to the

Good Hope Hospital. Entering the hall, they anxiously inquired for their friends.

"Mrs Donnelly is doing very well," they were informed by the girl at the desk. "Unfortunately, we can't say as much for Miss Chapelle. She has been seriously injured, and has lost a great deal of blood."

The girls were led into Mrs Donnelly's room. The patient was overjoyed at seeing them.

"I couldn't sleep last night for worrying about you," the woman declared.

"And we spent the night worrying about you," Nancy smiled.

"I don't wonder you did, for I was whisked away to this hospital almost before I knew I had been hurt. I had just gone to the washroom when the crash came. I was thrown to the floor and must have lost consciousness. In any event, when I came to I was in a car being transported to this place. I learned later that I was the first person taken from the wreck."

"Are you feeling better?" Nancy inquired.

"Yes indeed. The doctor tells me I'll be able to leave here in a few days."

The girls talked with Mrs Donnelly a while longer. Presently a nurse came to warn them that they must not tire the patient by remaining over their allotted fifteen minutes.

"May we see Miss Chapelle?" Nancy asked when they were again in the corridor.

The nurse hesitated.

"If you wish to do so, you may go in for a minute or two, but that is all. Be careful not to excite her, for her condition is grave."

Nancy was shocked as she entered Miss Chapelle's

room. The writer, swathed in bandages, scarcely moved a muscle as the girls approached her bed. Yet as Nancy bent over the pale, wan face, a gleam of recognition flashed into the woman's eyes.

"I shall die—I know it. I am glad you came for there is something I must tell you."

Her voice dropped to a whisper. Nancy moved nearer so that she might not miss a word.

"It's the story of—" The woman faltered; she could not finish. She closed her eyes, completely exhausted.

"Don't try to tell me now," Nancy said compassionately.

Miss Chapelle made one last desperate attempt to speak, raising up her head.

"The message—in the hollow oak—" she muttered.

Then she dropped back upon the pillow, and lapsed into unconsciousness.

Nancy and her friends huddled in the barren corridor outside Miss Chapelle's room. Doctors and attendants went in and out, their faces tense.

"As long as the doctors keep working over her, she must be living," Bess declared with forced cheerfulness.

Just then the door opened and a nurse quietly stepped into the corridor. She walked rapidly towards the girls.

"How is she?" Nancy asked fearfully.

"We thought the end had come, but by some miracle she has rallied. She is sleeping quietly now, but of course the danger is not past. If you are acquainted with her friends or relatives, I suggest you wire them immediately."

Nancy was forced to acknowledge that she could not provide the hospital with the names. However, she was struck with a sudden thought.

"Miss Chapelle came from Hollywood. It's possible

that someone there knows of her family. Or, you might get in touch with one of the magazines for which she writes."

"Thank you for your suggestion," the nurse said gratefully. "We'll try both leads."

Since they could be of no assistance by remaining at the hospital, the girls returned to the Hamilton Hotel.

"What are our plans to be?" George asked gloomily, as they discussed matters in their room. "Do we return to River Heights?"

"We shouldn't go away and leave Mrs Donnelly," Nancy said. "Anyway, from what the nurse told me I rather think she'll be able to travel again in a few days."

"Then do you think we might go on to Canada?" Bess questioned eagerly.

"If Mrs Donnelly recovers fully I think we can; that is, if I get my deed back."

"Why not drive out to the Ranny farm this afternoon?" George proposed.

"I had thought of it. We're not doing any good here, and the excursion will help fill in our time."

The girls decided to hire a car to drive themselves. However, they were less enthusiastic about the idea when they saw the old car that was assigned to them.

"Do you think it will hold together long enough for us to get to the Ranny farm?" Bess asked doubtfully.

"That car's been running for nearly ten years now," the owner informed her, irritated by her manner. "You're the first that ever complained about it."

"Oh, we're not complaining," Nancy said hastily. "If you'll show me how to start the engine, I think we can manage very well."

Bess and George refused to have anything to do with

the intricate mechanism of the old vehicle, so Nancy was obliged to take the wheel. Before leaving town she inquired the way to the Ranny farm.

"Take the first turn south," she was told glibly, "then turn north at Fisher's farm, cross the Little Bear Creek, go south again for a bit, and angle off to the west until you come to a crooked lane. Follow it for maybe a mile, and you'll be there!"

"Just as clear as mud," Nancy laughingly reported to her chums. "I suspect this trip will turn out to be a pioneering expedition after all."

Before they had gone two miles a rear tyre blew out. It took the girls almost three-quarters of an hour to fix it, for some of the necessary tools were missing. When the tyre had been changed, they had difficulty in starting the car again, but at last the engine began to roar and the girls continued down the dusty road. They had no way of knowing how far they had travelled, for the speedometer was broken.

"It seems to me we've gone at least ten miles," George maintained. "I know we've taken a wrong turn somewhere."

"I suppose we have," Nancy sighed, stopping the car. "I think I'll walk over to that farmhouse on the hill and get directions."

Unwilling to be left behind, Bess and George insisted on walking with her. They crawled under a fence and struck out across the fields. Only after they had gone quite a distance did they notice a bull quietly grazing at the far end of the first field.

"O-oh," Bess squealed in fright, "let's turn back!"

"That old bull won't hurt you," George teased. "He isn't even looking this way."

But as she spoke the animal raised its head. With a snort of rage, it came towards the girls.

"Run for your lives!" Nancy shouted.

The three girls raced madly for the fence. Heavy hoofs pounded behind them. As she glanced over her shoulder, Nancy saw that soon the bull would be upon them. They might reach the fence, but they would not have time to climb over it.

"Hurry, and you'll make it!" a man's voice shouted.

The girls noticed a big wooden gate, and could see a farmer who was swinging it open for them. They darted through, collapsing at his feet. Then the gate slammed after them, and they were safe.

"What do you mean by frightening my bull?" the man demanded crossly.

The girls stared at him, then burst into laughter.

"We thought it was the other way round," Nancy managed to say, as she tried to regain her breath.

"Didn't you see that sign on the fence that said to keep out?"

"We didn't see any sign," Nancy maintained. "We were driving along the road and noticed your house. We wanted to ask the way to the Ranny farm, and thought we'd take a short cut through the field."

It was the farmer's turn to stare.

"You're at the Ranny farm now," he said.

"And are you Mr Ranny?" Nancy questioned. "The man who left the letter at the newspaper office?"

"Yes, I am. Who are you?"

Nancy told him her name and introduced her friends. The farmer softened considerably after they explained their mission.

"Yes, I have the paper safe in the house," he

*Ominously the bull started to move towards them . . .*

admitted. "I was taking the milk and some produce to town early in the morning, when I saw it lying on the grass. Soon as I looked at it I knew it was something important, so I wrote that letter and left it at the newspaper office. You're welcome to the paper if it belongs to you."

"Oh, thank you," Nancy said gratefully. "I can prove that it is mine, for it is a deed to property in Canada."

"Come along, then, and I'll give it to you."

He led the girls into a comfortable cottage and introduced them to a stout, pleasant-faced woman. She greeted the girls cordially, chatting amiably with them while her husband found the deed.

"A dreadful crash, wasn't it?" Mrs Ranny began conversationally.

"Indeed it was," Nancy agreed. "We were in it, too."

She then told of their experiences. The farmer's wife listened spellbound.

"I feel so sorry for the poor passengers who were hurt," Mrs Ranny said sympathetically. "I only wish we might do something to help."

"Perhaps you can," Nancy returned, as a plan occurred to her. Before she could tell what it was, Mr Ranny came with the deed.

"Here you are, Miss Drew. I'm glad to be able to help you."

"I wish you would accept a reward."

The farmer shook his head stubbornly, so Nancy did not urge him further.

Nancy was eager to show her gratitude for the return of the lost deed. As she prepared to leave, she mentioned the plan which had occurred to her.

"You spoke of wanting to do something to help the passengers who were injured in the crash, Mrs Ranny. As it happens, we have a friend who was slightly hurt. She is at the Good Hope Hospital now but expects to leave within a day or two. She should go to a place where she can have a complete rest. If you would care to have her here, I am sure that some arrangement might be worked out."

"I should indeed be glad to have her here," Mrs Ranny said without an instant's hesitation. "I don't mind saying we need money. And this is a quiet place for an invalid. We have plenty of milk and eggs."

"Then I'll talk over the idea with her and let you know," Nancy promised, turning to leave.

When Mrs Donnelly was informed of the plan, she was enthusiastic. Although Miss Chapelle's condition remained unchanged, the older woman had improved rapidly. The doctors agreed that she might leave the hospital whenever she wished.

At three the next afternoon a comfortable car brought Mrs Donnelly and the girls to the Ranny farm. Nancy was delighted to find that the invalid seemed highly pleased with the surroundings. However, when Mrs Ranny came hurrying out of the house to greet the party, the girl was destined for a severe shock.

"Mrs Ranny, this is Mrs Donnelly," said Nancy pleasantly.

The only response to her introduction was a chilly silence. The two women were staring at each other, bitter hatred in their eyes.

"Take me back to the hospital!" Mrs Donnelly ordered sharply. "Never in the world will I stay here!"

# ·6·

## The Message in the Hollow Oak

SUDDENLY Nancy realized that by bringing Mrs Donnelly to the home of Mrs Ranny she had unwittingly committed a grave error. Undoubtedly an old feud existed between the two women. Where they had met, or what had caused the trouble she had no idea; yet there was no question but that at the present moment the two were bitter enemies.

"Take me away from here!" Mrs Donnelly commanded.

Nancy ordered the driver to go back to the Hamilton Hotel. For some time the little party rode in silence, the girls waiting for Mrs Donnelly to offer some excuse for her strange behaviour. For several minutes she stared straight ahead and said nothing, but finally spoke.

"I never expected to see her again in my life," she murmured.

The girls waited expectantly. Then she went on, a slightly bitter note in her voice:

"Her father and mine were rivals years ago at Wellington Lake. They had trouble over a piece of timber land."

"And is that the reason why you harbour this ill feeling towards Mrs Ranny?" Nancy probed gently.

"Mrs Ranny? Is that her name now? I knew her

when she was a girl—neither of us was married at the time. It was natural that we should dislike each other when our fathers were at such daggers drawn. Probably the fight would never have been so bitter had it not been for money. But when gold is involved, people lose all sense of balance."

"Gold?" Nancy inquired alertly.

"Yes. The timber land I mentioned is very near yours. But please don't ask me to go into detail about it now. Meeting that woman after all these years has upset me dreadfully. I don't like to talk about it."

Nancy longed to ask questions about the old feud between the two families, and wanted to learn more about the competition for the timber land, but she carefully restrained herself. She could tell that Mrs Donnelly had been greatly unnerved by the incident.

"You must go to bed as soon as I can get a room for you," Nancy told her. "This long drive from the hospital has been too much of a strain on you."

"I feel exhausted. If I could just get some sleep——"

"You shall. Now, don't give Mrs Ranny another thought," the girl added, as they reached the hotel.

Nancy did not leave her until the woman had calmed down sufficiently to go to sleep. Then she returned to her friends, and the three discussed the situation together.

"I cannot work out how we'll ever manage to go on to Wellington Lake," Bess said gloomily. "After this setback Mrs Donnelly may be unable to travel for a week."

"The meeting with Mrs Ranny was unfortunate, to say the least," Nancy acknowledged. "Still, Mrs Donnelly looked much better when I left her. I believe after another day she'll be quite like herself again."

"There's still Miss Chapelle to think of," George reminded her friend. "What are you going to do about her?"

Nancy had not forgotten her new friend. Unbeknown to Bess and George, she had left word at the hospital that should the writer experience the slightest turn for the worse, they were to notify her at once.

"I couldn't leave here until I was sure Miss Chapelle was out of danger," Nancy told her friends soberly. "I took a great liking to her. Besides she's all alone."

Bess and George nodded in agreement.

"I guess we're all fretting because of the delay," Nancy went on in a more animated tone. "It seems I can't wait until we reach Canada! If there should be gold on the land——"

"That phrase has been your theme song ever since we left River Heights," George laughed.

"Gold can bring about a great many complications," Bess commented. "You've just seen how it has caused a bitter feud between Mrs Donnelly and Mrs Ranny."

"It seems a pity that they are estranged," Nancy murmured. "Of course, we may not know the whole story, but often serious quarrels develop from mere trifles."

It was almost time for a mail delivery. After discussing the situation a little longer, the girls went down to the lobby. They did not really expect any letters, so were pleasantly surprised when the clerk handed each of them a fat envelope.

"Word from home!" Nancy cried joyfully, dropping down onto the nearest chair to read the lengthy communication which her father had sent.

Carson Drew had added a brief note of warning to his long letter.

"Be sure," he wrote, "to keep a sharp lookout for Tom Stripe and Raymond Niles. I have reason to believe that they have left River Heights."

Nancy re-read the paragraph, remembering that Bess had maintained she had seen Niles at the time of the crash. Had the men planned to follow her to Canada? The thought troubled her.

"Why are you scowling?" George demanded with a laugh. "Bad news from home?"

Nancy's face relaxed.

"No, I was just thinking about something—nothing important."

The girls were starting towards the lift, when the clerk motioned to them to return to the desk.

"A telephone call for you, Miss Drew," he said.

Nancy went into a nearby booth. As she lifted the receiver she found herself connected with the Good Hope Hospital.

"Miss Drew, you asked us to notify you if Miss Chapelle's condition had changed. We should like you to come to the hospital at once."

"Has she taken a turn for the worse?" Nancy inquired anxiously.

"Yes. The doctors have decided to operate. It's the only hope they have of saving her life. She wants to talk to you before she undergoes the operation."

"I'll be there in a few minutes," Nancy promised.

She returned to her friends, and quickly explained to them the situation.

"I must leave at once. Perhaps you two should stay with Mrs Donnelly in case she needs someone."

"We'll look after her," George promised. "Oh, I do hope Miss Chapelle recovers from her operation."

Fifteen minutes later Nancy reached the hospital, and was sent directly to the upper floor, where she was met by the nurse who led the way down the silent corridor. Opening the door to Miss Chapelle's room, she motioned to Nancy to enter.

Nancy moved quietly to the bedside of the injured writer. A faint smile flickered over Miss Chapelle's wan face as she recognized the girl.

"I sent for you because there is something I have to tell you," Miss Chapelle began with difficulty.

"If anything should happen to me—will you promise to deliver a message to my grandfather? And to someone else whom I love dearly?"

"Of course, but I feel sure there will be no need for it. You will recover in a little while and be able to take the message yourself."

Miss Chapelle shook her head sadly.

"I fear that I shall never see Canada again."

"Canada?" Nancy questioned. "But I thought your home was in Hollywood."

"For years it has been. However, I was born in Canada. My real name is Annette Chap, although few people know it. My parents died when I was only six years old. Until I was sixteen I made my home with my grandfather, Pierre Chap."

"And is he still living in Canada?" Nancy probed gently.

"I have not heard any news of him for many years. I do know that if he is still living, his home is in the same log cabin. It is fifteen miles from Lake Wellington, deep in the woods. Anyone can direct you there."

"If he is still alive, I'll find him," Nancy promised.

A faraway expression crept into Annette Chap's misty grey eyes.

"Grandfather Pierre must be over seventy, but he has always been healthy and strong. How I should love to see him again!"

"You will, I feel sure."

"No, we are estranged. I ran away from home when I was only sixteen."

The woman lapsed into silence. Presently she continued, speaking with increasing difficulty:

"I was inclined to be a romantic youngster, and I fell in love with a young man named Norman Ranny."

Nancy started upon hearing the familiar surname, but the writer did not notice her sudden movement.

"Grandfather thought I was too young to have boy friends," she went on. "He hated Norman, and threatened to disown me if I were ever to marry him. Finally, we decided to elope."

Miss Chap slumped back against the pillows, and for a time appeared too weak to continue her story. But she forced herself to go on.

"We agreed, Norman and I, to carry on a correspondence using as a letter box the old oak tree."

"The hollow oak you mentioned before?" Nancy asked.

"Yes. There was one more than a hundred years old. In its trunk was a hollow which only Norman and I knew about. We used it as a hiding-place for our messages. I promised Norman that when I set the day for our elopement I would leave word for him in the hollow oak."

"And did you?"

"Yes, I wrote the message, saying I would meet him in a small town in the States just over the border."

"And did Norman meet you?" Nancy inquired.

"No," Miss Chap returned, a strained look coming over her face. "I stayed in the town for two days, but he didn't come. After that I was afraid to return to my grandfather. No doubt I made a great mistake, but I was very proud. I felt I could never bear facing Norman again."

"Perhaps he did not receive the message," Nancy suggested.

"I thought of that possibility later," Miss Chap confessed. "At any rate, I then went to Hollywood. I had a very hard time for many years, until success finally came. Now I have plenty of money. When I met you on the train I was on my way back to Canada to find my grandfather, and beg his forgiveness."

"Have you heard from Norman since you left your home?"

"Only indirectly. I have been told that he is still unmarried. I know that he served in the army, but I have no idea where he is living at present. I should like to see him again, but I fear that will never be."

"Don't feel so discouraged," Nancy urged. "The operation will be a success."

"I hope so," Miss Chap said, smiling faintly. "But I have no real hope, so that's why I sent for you. The story I have just told you has been incorporated in my new novel. It is the best work I have ever done, for it is really the story of my life. If somehow you can find my grandfather and tell him the truth about me, I shall be eternally grateful to you."

"I gladly accept the trust," Nancy promised seriously.

Miss Chap relaxed slightly.

"Now I shall rest easier. You have been very kind."

The door suddenly opened and a nurse came in.

"I'm sorry, but you'll have to leave now," she said to Nancy. "It's time to take Miss Chapelle to the operating theatre."

A slight shudder passed through the writer as she realized that the ordeal was so near at hand. But she smiled bravely as Nancy bent down to kiss her.

"Keep up your courage," the girl whispered, a warm smile on her face.

She remained in the corridor until she saw the attendants wheel the white-robed figure towards the operating theatre. After arranging with the nurse that she be informed of Miss Chapelle's progress, Nancy left the hospital but did not return immediately to the Hamilton Hotel. Instead, she telephoned Bess and George and asked them to meet her at the Ranny farm.

"We'll get there as soon as we can," George promised. "But why are you in such a hurry?"

Nancy said she would explain everything later. She was waiting at the lane which led to the farm cottage when the girls drove up in a hired car.

"I'd have returned to the hotel for you, but time was so short," Nancy apologized. "Miss Chapelle told me her real name as well as the story of her life. I think I have a clue as to what became of her former sweetheart. By the time she recovers from the operation I hope to have some good news for her."

"You're talking in absolute riddles," Bess announced, as the three hurried towards the house on the hill.

"I suppose I am," Nancy admitted, laughing. "I'm so excited that my thoughts are going round in a fearful whirl. Oh, if I could only find Norman, how wonderful that would be!"

"Norman?" George demanded.

"Norman Ranny. I have a hunch that he may perhaps be related to these Rannys!"

As the girls walked up the winding lane, Nancy told her friends the main facts of Miss Chapelle's story. Bess and George grew excited.

"After all that occurred here as a result of our bringing Mrs Donnelly, we may not be received very well," Bess remarked uneasily.

"I think Mrs Ranny will talk to us," Nancy insisted. "It wasn't our fault that she and Mrs Donnelly were involved in a feud."

The farm woman did not bear the girls any ill-will. When they knocked at her door she bade them enter in as cordial a manner as ever.

"I know why you have come," she said before Nancy could speak. "It is kind of you to offer to help patch up the trouble between Mrs Donnelly and myself, but that is quite impossible."

"I have come on an entirely different mission," Nancy told the woman. "I should like to know if by any chance you have a son named Norman?"

A queer expression flickered over Mrs Ranny's face. "Yes, I have."

Nancy was elated.

"Then tell me where I can find him," she pleaded. "I must see him at once!"

"I don't know where he is."

# ·7·

## Nancy's Mission

"I DON'T know where my son is just at present," Mrs Ranny repeated reluctantly.

"Have you any idea when he will return home!" Nancy questioned eagerly.

"No, he often goes and comes without explaining his whereabouts to me. Since he was in the army Norman has changed so that we hardly know him as the same person he used to be."

"Did he ever marry?"

"His sweetheart disappointed him, and he never fully recovered from the shock."

By this time Nancy was almost convinced that the Norman whom she was seeking was none other than Mrs Ranny's son. She longed to tell the woman the entire story, yet hesitated to do so, for the secret was not hers to divulge. It would be best, she decided, to make a quiet investigation before revealing what she had learned.

"Could you give me a picture of your son?" she next inquired of Mrs Ranny. "Preferably one taken before he went into the army?"

"Yes, I believe I have an old picture of him," Mrs Ranny agreed a trifle unwillingly. "Wait and I'll look."

She went over to a desk, and after rummaging through several drawers found an old faded photograph which she gave to Nancy.

The face which Nancy saw was not strictly handsome, but the well-defined features denoted strength of character.

"This should do," the girl announced. "May I borrow it for a few days? I promise to be careful with it and return it as quickly as possible."

Obviously, Mrs Ranny did not wish to lend her the photograph. However, she could think of no graceful way to refuse. While the woman was still debating the matter, Nancy thanked her again and hurried away.

"Poor woman, you frightened her almost to death," Bess remarked as they sped back to the hotel.

"I didn't want to worry her," Nancy returned, "but I just had to get that picture."

Back at the hotel the girls found Mrs Donnelly considerably improved. She was rocking restlessly in her chair as they came into her bedroom.

"I've been thinking that we may as well go on to Wellington Lake," she announced abruptly. "I don't like this place, and I'm eager to get home. I'll convalesce there a lot faster than I will here."

"But are you really able to travel?" Nancy asked solicitously.

"Fiddlesticks! Of course I am. That Ranny woman upset me a little, I admit, but aside from that I'm as well as I ever was!"

Nancy smiled at this contradictory speech, for Mrs Donnelly had not yet fully recovered from her injuries. However, the girls felt that once she had made up her mind to travel, nothing would keep her from it.

Nancy thought it best not to tell Mrs Donnelly Miss Chapelle's story, since it concerned the Rannys. Secretly, she was eager to arrive at Wellington Lake as soon as possible so that she might fulfil the promise she had made.

"I believe we can get a fast train out of here in about an hour," she said.

"Then have your luggage ready," the old lady advised crisply. "I packed my bag over an hour ago. I am sick and tired of this hotel, and we can't leave it too soon for me!"

Elated at the thought of pressing on to Wellington Lake, Nancy hustled about making all the necessary arrangements.

Once on the train that evening, Nancy saw to it that Mrs Donnelly was comfortably settled in her berth. Then with her friends she retired to the observation coach to read a magazine.

"I wonder how Miss Chapelle is getting along?" Bess meditated. "It was too bad we didn't have another chance to see her before we left."

"Yes," Nancy agreed, "but the nurse told me that after the operation she would be unable to have visitors for several days. I feel that I can help her best by going on to Wellington Lake."

Until the last gleam of daylight remained, the girls sat out in the observation coach, admiring the rugged scenery. The hillsides along the tracks were thick with jackpine. The fragrant air was steadily growing cooler.

"Time to turn in," George suggested as the hour grew late.

"I'm as drowsy as an old tabby cat," Bess yawned. "It must be the change of air."

The cousins rose to go to their berths. Nancy, however, lingered behind.

"I'll be along in a minute or two," she promised.

For almost an hour she remained alone, listening to the monotonous click of the wheels over the rails. She felt thrilled and excited. Lake Wellington! What a magic sound!

"I'll be there tomorrow," she told herself over and over. "Perhaps I'm foolish, but I can't help but feel that besides aiding Miss Chapelle, I'm to have a glorious holiday as well!"

At eight o'clock the following morning Nancy was re-strapping her bag, when George burst in to tell her that the train was rapidly approaching their destination.

"I'm all ready, George. I'll be with you in a second."

Ten minutes later the train pulled into Wellington Lake. Mrs Donnelly had telegraphed ahead that she was coming, so a car was waiting to take them all to her boarding house.

"Well, girls, what do you think of the country?" she asked cheerfully when they were in the car. "Pretty, isn't it?"

"The town of Wellington Lake is beautiful," Nancy told her truthfully. "I love the smell of the pines."

"We're coming to the water now," the old lady announced as they rounded a bend in the road. "Did you ever see anything so blue?"

"Never!" Bess gasped, surveying the lake in awe.

"The fishing is good here, too," Mrs Donnelly went on proudly. "Toss in a hook almost anywhere, and you'll catch perch or pike. Plenty of trout, too."

"I believe I'll have very little time in which to fish," Nancy said doubtfully. "I want to look over my property, and I must also visit some people who live about fifteen miles from here."

Mrs Donnelly looked up alertly, but it was not in her nature to ask questions.

"If you go into the woods you'll need a guide," she advised. "This is rough country, and the farther you get from Lake Wellington the rougher it becomes."

The woman's boarding house deserved a more elegant name. It was a large building made of logs, which nestled in a setting of tall pines. The interior was comfortably furnished. Glowing embers smouldered in a great open fireplace.

A woman whom Mrs Donnelly termed the "hired girl" had breakfast waiting for them.

"I don't wonder you were eager to get here," Nancy smiled, taking a third helping of pancakes. "The food is delicious."

"You're nibbling at those flapjacks like a little bird! Wait until you've been here a week—then you'll eat hearty!"

After breakfast Bess and George went straight to their rooms. Nancy, however, had glimpsed a local paper on the living room table, and lingered to glance over it. Suddenly she caught sight of a familiar name, and eagerly read every word of the item. It told of a bad storm which had struck the district directly north of Wellington Lake. A stranger seated under a huge old oak tree on the Pierre Chap property had narrowly escaped death when a large bough had been snapped off.

"I wonder if that could be the tree Miss Chapelle told me about!" Nancy asked of herself excitedly. "The old 'letter-box' oak! Early tomorrow I shall go there."

## ·8·

## Into the Woods

THE next morning at breakfast Nancy spoke of her desire to visit the Chap property. She was relieved when Mrs Donnelly offered some practical advice without asking leading questions.

"Pete Atkins is one of the best guides in this part of the country. For a very reasonable sum he'll provide you with a boat and all necessary equipment, as well as cook your lunch for you."

"Must we go by boat?" Nancy asked in surprise.

"That would be the only sensible way. The Chap property has a rough road leading up to it, but I know you would find the route tedious. By boat you will have a far more enjoyable time."

"I think the water trip would be lots of fun," George remarked.

"Well, hardly that," Mrs Donnelly smiled, "for you must make two treks between lakes. However, it will be a worthwhile experience."

"How can we get in touch with Pete Atkins?" Nancy inquired.

"I'll make all the arrangements for you if you wish. When would you want to start?"

"As soon as possible."

Mrs Donnelly glanced at the clock.

"It's late now, but if Pete works fast you might get away by nine o'clock. That should give you ample time to reach your destination before nightfall."

"Then we'll not return until tomorrow," Nancy told her. "I won't know how long I'll be detained until after I get there."

"I'll not worry about your safety as long as Pete Atkins looks after you," Mrs Donnelly assured her.

Arrangements were soon completed, and the girls went to their rooms to dress for the trip. When the guide met them at the boat landing, he nodded approvingly as he saw that they wore slacks and boots.

"Take good care of my girls," Mrs Donnelly cautioned him.

"The best ever," he grinned.

Pete had brought along a small motorboat. As the little boat shot across the lake the girls thought that the journey was to be both a rapid and a pleasant one. They soon arrived at the start of the first trek, and there the boat was left behind.

"We'll carry only paddles and the grub," Pete explained as they set off through a narrow forest trail. "I have a canoe hidden at Lake Stewart."

Each of the girls had a light pack to carry. Before they had gone a mile, however, their burdens seemed to weigh twice as much. They were overjoyed and relieved when they came within view of sparkling blue water again.

Pete drew out a red canoe from the bushes where it had been cleverly hidden. Bending over to launch it, he gazed with interest at a fresh footprint in the sand.

"Someone's been through here this morning," he observed briefly. "City fellow, too."

M ɪ

"How can you tell?" Bess whispered curiously.

"Type of shoe," Nancy answered.

Pete helped the girls into the boat, and did not refer again to the footprint. However, as she sat in the bow helping to paddle, Nancy wondered idly who could have made it.

Her thoughts turned to Grandfather Chap. Would she find him at home and in good health? How disappointing it would be if she were to fail in her mission!

As she suddenly scanned the dazzling waters she observed a small moving object directly ahead. It was a boat. She pointed out the craft to the guide, but his sharp eyes had noted it long before she had. They dipped their paddles deeper, and gradually drew closer to the boat.

"It looks to me as if they're trying to keep well ahead of us," Nancy commented, a trifle puzzled.

Two men were in the canoe. Both of them handled their oars awkwardly. Nancy did not expect to recognize either of them, and therefore was greatly surprised when one of them glanced back and she caught a glimpse of his face.

"Why it's Tom Stripe, I do believe!" she exclaimed.

The guide's face was as black as a thunder cloud.

"Do you know him?" Nancy demanded.

"He's been up here before," Pete snapped. "A nasty character, if there ever was one!"

Nancy watched the boat closely. Unless she was greatly mistaken, Stripe's companion was none other than Raymond Niles! Had the two men purposely followed her to Wellington Lake? She was afraid that trouble lay ahead of her.

The two men were aware that they had been seen,

and accordingly took to their oars with a will. Soon they had disappeared behind a bend in the lake, where they were hidden from view. When Nancy and her party reached the spot a few minutes later, they saw no sign of the other boat.

"That's queer," she murmured. "I wonder where those men could have gone!"

Her eyes swept the shore, but the canoe was nowhere to be seen. However, it would be a very simple matter to conceal the craft among the dense bushes and pine trees that lined the water.

"Perhaps Niles and Stripe came up here only to fish," Bess observed optimistically. "Mrs Donnelly told me this is one of the best fishing places in Canada."

"They won't get much of a catch by hiding in the bushes," the guide returned grimly.

Although Nancy and her chums surveyed the lake at intervals, they did not again catch sight of the two men. After an uneventful hour had passed they relaxed slightly.

"I'm hungry as a bear," George presently remarked.

Pete acknowledged this remark with a smile, and pointed the canoe towards shore.

"We may as well stop for lunch. This is as good a place as any."

They pulled the craft up on to the sandy beach and unloaded their knapsacks. The girls looked on admiringly as Pete built a fire. Then he took out a battered coffee pot and a smoke-blackened skillet. Soon the air was fragrant with the odour of bacon and potatoes frying.

The girls were ashamed of the amount of food they were able to consume. At home they might have scorned such simple fare, but after the morning's paddle even coarse bread tasted delicious.

"I'll go to the spring for some fresh water, and then we'll start on again," Pete announced after they had finished.

Nancy and her chums were clearing away the rubbish, when they were startled at hearing a slight noise in the bushes.

"Who's there?" Nancy called out sharply.

Tom Stripe and Raymond Niles stepped out into the open.

"What do you want?" Nancy demanded.

"Oh, just a little talk with you," the latter said blandly. "We're interested in that newly-acquired property of yours."

"So I suspected!"

"Now don't get up on your high-horse," Niles wheedled. "We're not trying to cheat you out of anything."

"I wish I could be sure of that."

"We're perfectly willing to pay you a good price for your land."

"What price?" Nancy questioned shrewdly.

"The land cost you nothing, so anything you might make is clear profit. Now the property is barren—practically valueless. It will cost you more in taxes than it is worth. Considering all this, we feel that two hundred dollars would be more than a fair sum."

Nancy could not repress a smile.

"If the land is so worthless, why do you want to buy it!"

"It is located not far from a good fishing lake. We hope to build a cabin there."

"I don't care to sell," Nancy said coldly.

"You're making a mistake," Tom Stripe snarled.

"I think I'm not!" Nancy retorted, angered by the surly tones. "If you must know the truth, I distrust both of you!"

"We want the land, and we'll get it, too!" Stripe fairly shouted. "If you won't sell to us, we'll leave you stranded! We'll wreck your canoe!"

In sudden rage he darted towards the shore where the craft had been left. Nancy and her friends pursued him, but Raymond Niles blocked their way. Stripe pushed the light canoe out into the water, and overturned it.

"Pete! Help!" Nancy shouted frantically.

Their guide came running down the trail. With one leap he was upon Tom Stripe.

The men struggled knee-deep in water. Then, with a mighty blow, Pete struck the man under the chin. He reeled backwards, lost his balance and toppled over into the water.

Nancy had not remained idle. Raymond Niles held her arms, but she struggled valiantly to free herself. Just as Stripe pitched backwards she jerked away, taking her captor completely by surprise. Then she gave him a powerful shove. He stumbled and tried to save himself, but failed. With a yell of rage he, too, fell into the water.

For an instant Nancy stood watching the two men as they struggled to regain their footing. Then it dawned upon her that she and her friends were missing a golden opportunity to make their getaway.

"Quick!" she shouted to her companions. "Help me right the canoe!"

# ·9·

## Tricked!

BESS and George were too startled to obey, but Pete splashed out into the lake to help Nancy recover the floating craft. With a deft movement they flipped out most of the water from the canoe.

By this time the cousins had caught up the knapsacks, and now jumped into the boat which Pete steadied for them. As soon as Nancy was in, he took his own place at the stern. Three mighty sweeps of the paddle, and the four were well beyond reach of Niles and Stripe, who stood glaring after them.

"I'll get even with you for this!" the latter shouted, shaking his fist.

"If I ever see you again, I'll give you a worse ducking!" Pete called back.

With the craft rapidly drawing farther and farther from shore, pursuit was out of the question. The bedraggled men gloomily returned to their abandoned campfire where they piled the wood high and tried to dry their wet clothes.

As he was looking round for more logs, Tom Stripe noticed a slip of paper lying on the ground. Curiously he picked it up. His face brightened at the sight of it, for it was a note which Nancy had unwittingly dropped during her scuffle with Niles.

The paper gave complete instructions for reaching the Chap cabin.

"We're in luck after all!" he said to his companion excitedly. "Nancy Drew wasn't so smart when she dropped this."

"Let's see it," Niles commanded.

His eyes gleamed as he read the directions.

"It's a dead give-away as to where she's going, Tom."

"Sure, and if we could just beat her there."

"They have the head start. That Pete Atkins paddles like a machine!"

Stripe's eyes narrowed.

"I know a trail that leads there, but it's hard going."

"Let's try it anyway. We have no chance by water. I'll stand a lot of punishment in order to get the best of Nancy Drew!"

Their clothing still damp, the two men set off through the woods. Stripe had not exaggerated when he said that the trail would be difficult. It was overgrown with vines and brush, but, intent on their purpose, they kept doggedly on their way.

"I'm getting sick of all this!" Niles announced in disgust after several hours of steady tramping. "It seems we should be getting there pretty soon. Tom, are you sure you know where we're going?"

"I thought I did. We may have taken the wrong fork back there a mile or so."

Niles glared at his companion as he wiped the perspiration from his grimy face.

"This is a fine time to decide you've made a mistake! I might have known you'd get me into a mess like this. We're in a fine pickle now! Lost in the wilderness, and not a living soul for miles around!"

"You're wrong about that, stranger," announced a voice from behind.

The men wheeled, to find themselves facing a bearded stranger who had quietly stepped out from among the bushes.

"Who are you?" Stripe demanded.

"Ranny is the name," the man informed him. "Norman Ranny."

Stripe and Niles had been quick to note that the newcomer carried prospecting tools.

"Is it true that there's gold around here?" Niles asked, a trifle tensely.

The man studied him coolly.

"Not here in the woods," he retorted.

"But along the streams?" Tom Stripe probed eagerly.

"Some say one thing, others say another," was the noncommittal reply.

"Could you give us a bite to eat and tell us how to get to old man Chap's place?" Niles questioned, realizing that it would do no good to ask about the gold. "We're hungry, and just about done for."

The prospector grew more friendly.

"You're not far from Pierre Chap's cabin now. If you want to come on to my place farther down the trail, I'll give you some food and show you the way."

"All right. Let's get going," Stripe urged. "We're eager to reach there."

"Why the hurry, stranger?" Norman Ranny inquired as he led the way down the trail. "Up here we try to take things as they come."

"Well, that isn't my way," Stripe responded stiffly. "If you won't point out the trail——"

"No need to be so quick on the trigger," the prospector drawled. "I'll show you the route all right. Only I thought you both looked tired and needed a rest."

"We do," Niles admitted. "We're trying to beat another party to old man Chap's, and we've been legging it as fast as we could possibly go."

Norman Ranny digested this information in silence. A little later they came within sight of a tiny cabin located in a clearing. The prospector flung the door wide open, and invited the men to enter.

"I'll fix something to eat," he offered. "It won't take me long."

The two sat down and looked curiously about them. The cabin was comfortably, though plainly furnished. The chairs and tables were substantial, home-made pieces of furniture. A pair of snowshoes and some animal skins decorated the bare walls. Over the bed hung a picture of a young girl.

"Nice looking dame," Niles commented familiarly.

Norman Ranny bent lower over the stove, as if he had not heard what had been said.

For want of anything else to do, Niles drew from his pocket the scrap of paper Nancy had dropped. After re-reading the directions, he carelessly tossed the note on to the table.

A minute later, in setting down a dish, Norman Ranny glanced at the paper. A name which Nancy had jotted down stood out and held his attention. He re-read it to make sure he was not mistaken.

"Annette Chap!"

The words seared his very brain! The name of his sweetheart!

"What's the matter?" Niles demanded suddenly. "You look sick."

Ranny stared at him almost stupidly.

"Where did you get this paper?" he questioned.

"Oh, from a girl," Niles told him carelessly.

"A girl," Ranny repeated, as if in a daze.

Niles and Stripe exchanged glances. What was wrong with the man? He acted as if he were not quite sane.

"Say, I think we'll not wait for food," Stripe said, rising quickly to his feet. "If you'll point out the way to old man Chap's we'll not trouble you any longer."

"And all the while I thought her dead——" the prospector muttered. "Could I have made a mistake?"

"What was that?" Niles demanded, bewildered.

With an effort the prospector forced himself to become aware of the two men.

"I am very sorry," he apologized. "I'll have dinner ready in a few minutes."

"But we said—" Defeated, Stripe sank back once more into his chair.

"It's no use," Niles warned his companion in a whisper. "He's out of his mind. We must humour him, or he may try to kill us."

The two crooks scarcely took their eyes off the man as he went on preparing the meal. Soon the food was ready. The men ate what the prospector set before them, but with little appetite.

Norman Ranny did not join them but sat staring moodily into space. When they had finished their meal the two men rose in obvious relief.

"Many thanks," Niles said, too heartily to sound sincere. "Now, if you'll point out the trail, Mr Ranny, we'll be on our way again."

The prospector also rose.

"I'll go with you," he said.

"There's no need for that," Stripe interposed hastily.

"It seems to me you don't care for my company, stranger."

"Oh, no, it isn't that," Niles said quickly. "Of course we want you to go, but we don't like to put you to so much trouble."

"No trouble at all. Come along. I'll lead the way."

Thoroughly disgusted, Niles and Stripe reluctantly followed their host from the cabin. It was not until they had gone some distance along the trail that they remembered the scrap of paper. Niles could not remember having seen it lying on the table as they had left the cabin.

He glanced curiously at their guide. Had Ranny picked it up? Shrugging his shoulders, Niles abandoned the problem.

"Maybe we can get away from him a little farther on," Stripe suggested in a whisper.

They waited hopefully for an opportunity, but whenever they lingered on the trail Norman Ranny stopped until they caught up again.

"We can't shake him," Niles whispered irritably. "No use in trying."

Soon they came to a large clearing with a small cabin surrounded by cultivated fields. About three hundred yards from the house stood an old mill.

"Chap has a nice place here," the prospector said quietly. "He cleared all the land himself."

"Well, thanks for showing us the way," Stripe remarked pointedly.

Norman Ranny made no move to depart. "I may

as well wait around here and see if anyone is at home."

Infuriated, the two men stalked up to the front door, and knocked on it. There was no response so Niles knocked again.

"I thought he wouldn't be here," Norman Ranny said.

He watched the two men closely, and they could not help but see the suspicious look in his eyes. Exasperated, Stripe flung open the door that had been left unlocked.

"Look here," Norman Ranny protested, following them inside. "You can't break into a man's house like this!"

"Oh, can't we?" Stripe sneered.

Wheeling about, he leaped upon the surprised man, and knocked him to the floor. Niles helped by holding the victim down until his arms and legs could be tied.

"Put a gag in his mouth, too," Stripe advised, "or he'll be letting out a yell at the wrong time!"

His companion found an old towel which he stuffed between the prospector's teeth.

"I guess that will keep him safe for a while," he observed in relief. "No telling what he might have done to us if he'd had the chance."

"Chap may come back any minute," Stripe commented uneasily. "We'll have to hide this fellow somewhere."

Niles was peering into the dark basement.

"I think there's some sort of cellar down there," he said.

The two men carried the helpless prospector below, and locked him in a little stuffy room which Niles had discovered. Carefully they closed the entrance to the dungeon-like place and returned to the upper floor.

Scarcely had they recovered their breath than Niles, who was standing by the window, observed Nancy Drew and her party beaching their canoe on the lake shore.

"We were just in time, Tom. What's our next move?"

"We'll hide, and let them walk into our trap."

No sooner had the two hidden themselves than a knock was heard upon the door. This was repeated several times.

Niles and Stripe waited breathlessly, expecting that Nancy and her friends would soon give up and force their way in. But instead, Nancy gazed speculatively towards the old mill which stood at some distance from the house.

"Mr Chap may be working there," she suggested. "Shall we investigate?"

Not until she and her companions had reached the dilapidated old building did they see that it had not been used in recent years. The stream that fed the water wheel had entirely dried away.

"It isn't likely Mr Chap is here," George commented.

"After walking this far we may as well make sure," Nancy said.

She led the way towards the structure. Bess and George, attracted by the water wheel, stopped to look at it, and Nancy, going on, presently lost sight of the guide, also. She wandered alone through the machinery room and examined the granary.

Impelled by some impulse which she could not explain, she walked over to the decaying wall. Stooping over, she peered through one of the large cracks, and saw the cabin quite plainly. Tom Stripe was standing at the window, cautiously peering out.

Nancy could hardly believe her eyes. However, a second glance assured her that she had not been mistaken. Stripe and Niles had arrived ahead of her at the shack. For all she knew, they might have harmed Grandfather Pierre!

Hastily she returned to her friends, and in terse sentences reported to them what she had seen.

"They hope to take us by surprise," she said. "We must outwit them."

"But how?" George demanded.

In a few words Nancy outlined a plan. Bess and George were to circle to the rear of the cabin, being careful not to be seen. From the trees they were to watch Stripe and his companion.

"Pete and I will sneak back and hide the canoe."

"But I don't see what good that will do," Bess protested.

"I'm hoping that Niles and Stripe will notice that the craft is gone, and think that we left with it."

"That's an idea," George chuckled. "Come on, Bess. Better take off that bright sweater of yours. It's too conspicuous."

Keeping themselves well hidden by the bushes, Nancy and the guide stole down to the shore where they had beached the canoe. They directed a hasty glance towards the cabin to make sure their movements had not been observed, and then drew the boat far back into the undergrowth. Then they covered over the tracks leading to the hiding place, and moved on down the beach, making a wide circle back to the rear of the old house.

For a long time nothing happened, and Nancy felt herself growing discouraged.

"I guess it's no use," she said in disgust.

"Wait!" the guide directed, pulling her back into the bushes.

The door of the cabin slowly opened, and Raymond Niles peered cautiously out. He motioned to Stripe, and the two made their way stealthily down to the beach.

"Why, they've gone!" Niles exclaimed, observing the place where the canoe had been beached.

"That's queer," his companion muttered, looking about him. "I didn't see them leave."

"I lost sight of them when they went into the old mill," Niles added. "Wonder where they could have gone?"

"Not back to Wellington Lake, that's certain. Nancy Drew wouldn't give up so easily."

"You're right," Niles agreed. "Say, I'll bet that guide of hers knows where to find Chap."

"Likely as not he's gone to inspect Nancy Drew's new property. It adjoins his land, and he may have decided to buy it."

"Say, why didn't we think of that before?" Niles demanded. "I wondered why she was streaking way off here. Must be she has some arrangement with Chap about buying the land."

"That's why she wouldn't deal with us," Stripe growled.

The two men peered out over the lake, but there was no sign of the little red canoe.

"If we only had a boat we might overtake them," Stripe muttered. "I know the location of the land."

They glanced up and down the shore. As chance would have it, Pierre Chap had left his boat beached upon the sand only a hundred yards away. With one accord the two men ran towards it.

"They'll get good and tired before they've rowed that tub very far," the girls' guide chuckled, as he saw the men launch the craft. "It weighs a ton, and Pierre Chap doesn't use it any more."

After the boat was far out upon the lake, Nancy and Pete joined George and Bess, who had climbed a tall tree at the rear of the cabin and witnessed everything.

"Pierre Chap may be coming home soon," Nancy said thoughtfully, as the party considered its next move. "Maybe we ought to go inside the cabin and see how things are."

"I'll stay out of doors and keep watch," Pete offered, opening the door for the girls to enter. "Stripe and his friend may decide to come back. It's better to have someone remain on guard."

Nancy and her chums settled themselves comfortably inside the cabin, being careful all the while to disturb nothing. Everything was in order; only the breakfast dishes had not been washed.

"At least we know that Mr Chap has been here today," Nancy commented, "so it's quite likely that he'll return before dark."

After some time the girls grew tired of sitting around idly, so Bess suggested that they wash and dry the dishes.

"We may as well," George agreed. "It will help Mr Chap, and at the same time keep us from dying of boredom."

Bess heated some water on the little oil stove, and soon had some clean dishes for her friends to dry.

Nancy was putting them away in the cupboard when she abruptly halted, and listened intently.

"What's wrong?" George asked uneasily.

Nancy did not answer immediately.

"I thought I heard a noise but it was probably nothing," she finally responded.

"You must be imagining things," Bess laughed. "There is something eerie about this place—it must be the silence."

"I didn't hear a thing," George added. "It must have been——"

Her words ended in a surprised gasp, for a low groan seemed to issue from the very floor boards. "Did you hear that?" she whispered apprehensively.

"What could it have been?" Bess shuddered.

"It sounded like someone in pain," Nancy replied.

They huddled together, listening intently. A moment later they heard the strange noise again—a loud, unearthly moan.

"It's a ghost," Bess insisted, her teeth chattering with fright.

"There are no ghosts," Nancy returned firmly. But it took all her courage to add, "I'm going down to the cellar to find out just what it really is!"

Before she could move there was a loud crash that seemed to come from under their very feet.

"Oh! Oh!" Bess wailed.

Nancy rushed to the door.

"Pete! Pete!" she called.

There was no response to her cry. The guide had vanished!

# ·10·

## The Cellar Ghost

COURAGEOUSLY, Nancy lifted the trapdoor and peered down into the dark cellar.

"Wait for me at the head of the stairs," she directed. "I'm going to make a thorough investigation."

Cautiously she descended the steps, one at a time. It was so dark she could scarcely see a foot ahead of her. She groped her way along the wall, listening intently all the while. Then suddenly she heard the sound of soft breathing. Next there came an almost inaudible moan which seemed to come from a door in the corner.

Gathering her courage, the girl tried the door, but it would not open. Groping about in the musty darkness, she located the key in the lock and turned it. Opening the door a crack, she peered inside. At first she saw nothing, then gradually she could make out the figure of a man lying on the floor.

"Girls!" she shouted excitedly. "Come here! I think poor Mr Chap has been hurt!"

Bess and George dashed down the stairs to help her. They stared aghast as they beheld the bearded man lying trussed and gagged on the cold, hard floor.

"Get a knife to cut his bonds," Nancy urged.

George ran back to the kitchen while Nancy and Bess removed the gag from the man's mouth.

"We'll soon have you free," they encouraged him.

George came with the knife, and the thongs were quickly severed.

"Can you walk?" Nancy questioned the man anxiously, as they helped him to his feet.

"I think so," he responded with an effort.

Supporting him on either side, the girls assisted him up the stairs and into the kitchen. As the circulation improved in his numb limbs, he was able to walk more freely.

"Water," he pleaded.

Bess ran to get it. After the man had drunk deeply he smiled gratefully at the girls.

"I feel better now," he said, relieved.

Nancy studied his face intently.

"You can't be Pierre Chap," she declared, "you're far too young."

"I live some distance from here," the bearded prospector told her. "Two men stopped me on the trail and asked me the way to this place. I grew suspicious, and decided to come with them. They overpowered me and threw me into the cellar. If it hadn't been for your timely arrival I might have been here a long time."

"It must have been Tom Stripe and Raymond Niles who did it," Nancy surmised. "Can you describe your assailants?"

The prospector gave an accurate description of the two men.

"They should be arrested for this!" George cried indignantly. "When we return to Lake Wellington we'll report the matter to the police."

The prospector looked troubled.

"I'd rather you wouldn't," he said. "I'd prefer to even the score myself."

During the conversation Nancy had remained strangely quiet, though her chums noted that she stared at the stranger in a most peculiar manner. In truth, Nancy was bewildered. From the first the man had reminded her of someone, and vainly she racked her memory. Where had she seen him before?

Suddenly the answer came to her. Save for the beard, the stranger put her in mind of a photograph she had in her possession. Trying not to show her excitement, she turned to the prospector and asked him eagerly:

"Can it be possible that you are Norman Ranny?"

The stranger stared at Nancy in astonishment. For an instant she thought he intended to deny his identity, but he reluctantly nodded his head in assent.

"Yes, I am Norman Ranny. How did you know?"

"Your mother lent me your photograph," Nancy explained. "I also met Ann Chapelle, who told me her real name was Annette Chap."

The colour drained from the man's face.

"You have seen Annette?" he demanded, gripping Nancy's arm so tightly that it hurt her. "Then she is still alive?"

"Yes. When I last heard from the hospital she was slowly improving. She was seriously injured in a train crash and for some time the doctors feared she would not live. Even now she is not entirely out of danger."

"My poor Annette! If only I might go to her!"

"Can't you?" Nancy asked quietly.

"I am afraid she would not care to see me."

"I believe she still loves you," Nancy assured him.

Norman Ranny hung upon the girl's words, though he shook his head sadly.

"I should like to think so, but unfortunately I am unable to."

"Why do you say that?" Nancy inquired, puzzled at his attitude. "Surely it cannot be that you've changed in your feelings towards Miss Chap."

"I haven't changed in my regard for Annette," the man told her sincerely. "I have always loved her, and I always will."

"Then why can't you go to her now?"

"You don't understand. I have nothing to offer her. I am only a prospector—why, people here don't even know my real name. I thought it best to change it after I came out of the army."

"You have lived here ever since?" Nancy inquired.

"No. I visit my parents occasionally, and have stayed in many states and countries. There's something about this place that always draws me back. I guess it's because I knew Annette here."

Nancy nodded understandingly. Then the man went on, speaking brusquely to hide his emotions:

"When I was discharged from the army I was told that Annette had died. Until today I had no idea that she might still be alive."

"Tell me, do you ever visit the old hollow oak?" Nancy asked significantly.

"Yes, quite often. I was almost killed there two nights ago during a terrific storm. While I was sitting under the tree, a large bough snapped off."

"Then you were the stranger mentioned in the newspaper," Nancy commented.

"Yes. Here is the proof of it," the man smiled, pushing back his hair to reveal a deep gash in his scalp. "It was a wonder I wasn't killed. Not that it would have mattered greatly."

"Oh, you mustn't talk that way," Nancy said hastily.

"I can't help feeling the way I do. Life has never been worthwhile since I lost Annette."

"But wasn't it your own fault?" Nancy inquired gently.

"My own fault? What do you mean?"

"Didn't you ignore the message she left for you in the oak tree?"

Norman Ranny laughed shortly.

"I have been trying to forget it all my life."

"But why did you never meet her as she requested?" Nancy asked, exasperated.

"Meet her? The note said nothing about that."

"Didn't it state the town just over the border where she expected to join you?"

"It most certainly did not. Annette wrote me a very cold note. I recall the words. She said, 'I will not elope. I would rather have my grandfather's money.' "

"That isn't the way she explained it to me," Nancy gasped. "It must all have been a hoax! Perhaps someone changed the messages."

She then recounted everything Miss Chapelle had told her in the hospital.

"I can't understand it," he murmured after she had finished. "If I thought she was still waiting for me I'd go to her at once."

"I'm sure she is," Nancy told him.

"She wrote the note nearly nineteen years ago, and I know we have both changed greatly since that time. You tell me that Annette is now a successful novelist. But I have so little to offer her."

Nancy tried to persuade him that he was wrong. Though he listened closely to her words, they seemed to make no definite impression upon him.

"Had I known about the exchange of notes before I went into the army, everything might be different now," he said sadly. "Annette has her place in the city and I have my work here in the woods."

After a moment's silence Nancy asked:

"Do you often see Grandfather Chap?"

"Yes, though he does not know who I am. He became a recluse after his daughter ran away. He always ruled Annette with an iron hand, though he loved her dearly. Now he shuts himself up in his cabin."

"Have you any idea when Mr Chap will return?" Nancy asked him.

"Not the slightest. It begins to look as if he doesn't intend to come back here tonight."

Nancy and her chums looked troubled.

"We don't know what to do," George confessed. "Our guide has disappeared. We're stranded here."

"Who is your guide?"

"Pete Atkins."

"That's odd. He's as reliable a man as you'll find in these parts."

"We don't know what to make of it," Nancy admitted. "We brought along camping equipment, but it's very meagre."

"The nights are pretty cold here," Norman Ranny warned. "I could take you to the nearest town where you might find more comfortable quarters. I doubt if it will do us any good to stay here much longer."

"I suppose we should be starting out," Nancy said. After leaving a note for the guide in the event of his returning, Nancy and her friends followed the prospector a short distance through the dense timber until they arrived at a swiftly moving stream. From among the overhanging bushes the man drew forth a sturdy boat.

"This will be the quickest route," he stated, as he assisted the girls into the craft.

As they rowed down the stream, skilfully avoiding rocks and boulders, Nancy gave Ranny a description of the land she owned.

"It's not far from here," the prospector told her, "though it is in an even wilder section than this. Too bad you couldn't have inspected it."

"That's what I really wanted to do," Nancy admitted. "It's disappointing to have to leave without having seen it."

Ranny rested on his oars as he debated the situation.

"Well, why not turn round and go back?" he proposed. "I know a trapper and his wife with whom you might perhaps spend the night. In the morning you could continue on to your own property."

"Let's do it!" George declared enthusiastically. "After all, we made the trip to Canada for adventure!"

"Mrs Donnelly won't worry about us if we don't get back to Wellington Lake for several days," Bess added. Nancy required no urging to decide in favour of the trip, and gratefully accepted the prospector's generous offer to take them to the Dawson cabin. Norman Ranny directed the boat into a side stream, which was even swifter than the one they had previously taken. It required all his skill to keep them from being dashed against the rocks. Now and then a low-hanging bush would swish against the girls' cheeks, cutting like a whip.

"I can hardly wait until I see the land," Nancy declared excitedly. "How thrilled I'd be if there were gold on it!"

"That is the sustaining hope of every prospector," Ranny smiled. "But this property of yours sounds mighty good to me. I've found several big nuggets in Pebble Creek, which flows through your land."

"I'd love to see a nugget," Bess remarked.

Resting on his oars for a moment, Ranny took a small leather bag from his pocket and offered it to her. Somewhat awed, Bess withdrew several small lumps of gold, balancing them in the palm of her hand.

"I thought they would glitter more than this," she said.

Ranny laughed.

"They may not look like gold to you now," he said, "but they are, just the same."

"I hope we'll find a few nuggets on my property," Nancy said wistfully. "I'd like to take them home with me as souvenirs."

"I'll help you pan the stream if we have time," Ranny offered.

It was quite dark when the man finally guided the boat into a cove, and moored it. Through the trees the girls could see a light burning in a cabin. Ranny led the way, and in response to his knock a woman came to the door. She greeted him warmly, calling him by a name that was unfamiliar to Nancy and her friends.

"Come right in," she said, when she saw the girls. "We don' have many visitors, and we're always glad to entertain them."

"Sit in," Mr Dawson, the trapper, invited cordially, drawing up chairs for the girls. "The food's plain, but there's plenty of it."

Again the three girls were ashamed of their hearty appetites, though Mr and Mrs Dawson insisted that they were not doing full justice to the various dishes offered them. When Nancy tactfully suggested that she intended to pay for all the trouble she and her friends were causing, the couple refused to listen.

"Don't you give it a second thought," their hostess chuckled. "It's a treat for us to have you here."

In truth, the kindly people seemed to be enjoying the company of the girls, and plied them with innumerable questions about city life. After the supper dishes had been washed, the trapper brought out his banjo and played several gay, old-fashioned tunes.

"Our sons should be coming in before long," Mrs Dawson told Nancy. "Herman went to the nearest settlement for our monthly order of groceries. Jake, the older boy, started out to do some trout fishing."

As she spoke, the woman crossed over to the window to peer out. It troubled her that her boys had not yet returned.

"I can't understand what's keeping Jake," she remarked a little later. "It's too dark for him to be fishing now."

Ten minutes later footsteps could be heard outside. The door was flung open, and a youth, clad in the rough garments of a woodsman, staggered into the room bending low under the weight of a man whom he carried on his back.

"Jake!" Mrs Dawson cried, rushing to him. "What has happened?"

"I found him on the trail," he told his mother breathlessly, lowering the fellow to a couch. "He's badly hurt."

Nancy looked at the injured man. It was Pete Atkins!

# ·11·

## A False Claim

THE guide stirred restlessly on the couch as Nancy bent over him.

"Tom Stripe did it," he mumbled. "I'll get even!"

Mrs Dawson ran for a basin of warm water with which to sponge a gash on the victim's neck. A large bump stood out on the back of Pete's head, and Nancy suspected that the man had been struck from behind with a heavy club.

"I don't believe he's as badly hurt as it appeared at first," Norman Ranny said after they had attended to Pete. "If he gets a good sleep he should be all right in the morning."

"If he isn't, I'll go for a doctor," Jake offered.

Nancy and her friends were given a room for the night. Ranny and Jake, who did not mind sleeping in the open, rolled up in blankets outside. It was thought best not to move the guide from the couch, so Mr Dawson spent the night watching by his bedside.

In the morning Pete was considerably improved, though in no condition to endure the hardships of the trail. When Nancy questioned him as to what had happened, he offered little information.

"Tom Stripe and I have an old grudge. He got me

this time, but wait until we meet again!" was all he would say.

Although Nancy disliked leaving Pete behind, she realized he could hope for no better care than at the hands of the kindly Mrs Dawson. It seemed best that the girl go forward with her plans for viewing the newly-acquired land. Mr Dawson provided the party with horses, and his wife packed a lunch for them.

"You'll be perfectly safe with your new guide," she assured Nancy, smiling in Norman Ranny's direction. "There isn't a better woodsman in this part of the country than him."

Leaving the Dawson cabin, the party rode single file along a steep, rocky trail. Often their course would lead them beside some winding stream, where they paused to let their horses drink.

"Did you ever see such marvellous scenery before in all your life?" Bess demanded admiringly, as they paused at the crest of a pine knoll to gaze back towards the Dawson cabin. "Aren't you the lucky girl, Nancy, to own property in such a gorgeous district as this?"

"I'll not be very lucky if there isn't any gold here," Nancy laughed. "The land is so inaccessible for me it would be worthless for any other purpose."

At noon they halted near a waterfall for lunch, and after a brief rest continued their climb. An hour later Ranny, who was in the lead, drew up his mount and waited for the girls. With a sweep of his hand he indicated a fairly level stretch of land.

"Behold your property, Miss Drew!"

With a feeling akin to awe Nancy's eyes swept over the vast expanse of territory.

"All that—mine?"

"Land is cheap this far north," Ranny smiled. "But it won't be so for long—not if gold should be found here."

Slowly the group descended the knoll, and tied their horses to some trees near Pebble Creek.

"But where is the gold?" Bess queried in disappointment, as they walked about in the open stretches. "I haven't seen a single nugget!"

Norman Ranny laughed heartily.

"Did you expect to find them kicking around underfoot?" he asked.

"Well, I didn't know where to look," Bess returned defensively.

"If you like, we'll pan the creek," Ranny said. "I brought the necessary equipment."

"I want the first nugget," George cried gleefully.

The girls watched eagerly from the bank as the prospector panned for gold. At first it was exciting, but after a time the novelty of it wore off and they grew slightly tired of it.

"It doesn't look very promising," Bess commented wearily.

Just then Ranny took out a small object and tossed it over to Nancy.

"There's your nugget. It isn't worth much, but it's gold."

After that everyone wanted to try panning. The girls forgot all sense of time as they took turns using the equipment. Nancy found a similar lump of gold, while George, by diligent effort, acquired a slightly smaller one.

"I'm the only person that didn't get one," Bess grieved.

"Never mind. You may have the first one that was found," Nancy comforted.

While the girls had been engrossed at the stream, Ranny had wandered away to do a little prospecting on his own account. They came upon him working with his pick.

"Miss Drew, you may have something here after all," he said quickly as Nancy paused beside him. "The gold in the creek doesn't amount to much, but it looks to me as if I have struck a vein! Should that be the case, your fortune will have been made! If you like, I'll do some real prospecting here when I have more time."

Before Nancy could thank him for his friendly offer, a monotonous drone was suddenly heard coming from above. She peered upwards, to glimpse an aeroplane slowly circling over a large open stretch of land.

"Why, I believe it's going to land," she cried.

Fearfully they all watched as the plane sideslipped earthwards. A wing barely missed grazing the branch of a pine tree, which the pilot skilfully manœuvred to avoid.

The craft struck the narrow plot, and came bumping down over the rough ground. When it had come to a halt, two men leaped from the cockpit.

"What are you doing on private property?" one of them demanded of Ranny.

"This land belongs to me," Nancy maintained.

"Your claim is ridiculous," the other man snapped. "I am the owner of this ground. All of you must leave at once!"

Frightened, Bess and George backed away. Ranny and Nancy stood still.

"You are impostors!" the prospector shouted angrily. "I've seen your sort before."

He advanced menacingly, but Nancy placed a restraining hand upon his arm.

"Mr Ranny, you may have made a mistake about this being my property," she said. "After all, the boundaries weren't surveyed."

"I've made no mistake," the man retorted, his lips drawn in a thin, hard line.

The two newcomers ignored the little party, and began to stake out a claim. They selected the hillside where Ranny had been digging.

"I might have known what you were after," the prospector said in a threatening voice. "You're nothing but low-down thieves!"

A fight would doubtless have resulted, had not an interruption come. Another aeroplane loomed overhead. Everyone turned to look at it, as it slowly circled and presently landed beside the other one. Several men sprang out and began to unload mining machinery and equipment from the cockpit.

"There's no use in opposing them," Nancy warned Ranny. "They intend to steal my property. We can't prevent them, for they greatly outnumber us."

She felt sick at heart as she realized how she had been tricked. Not for an instant did she doubt that Tom Stripe and Raymond Niles were behind the scheme to steal her valuable mining land. She understood now why they had endeavoured to reach the property before she did.

One of the men whom the others addressed as Buck Sawtice presently advanced towards the girls. His attitude was decidedly menacing.

"We can't have you hanging around here," he said curtly. "You'll have to get off this claim. It belongs to the Yellow Dawn."

"Is that a company or a disease?" George asked sarcastically.

"It's a mining company, young lady. Now, if you don't want any trouble, get going!"

Nancy signalled her companions to offer no resistance. Taking their cue from her, they followed her across the field.

However, Carson Drew's daughter had no intention of abandoning the battle. She realized that it would be useless for her to get into a fight; if she wanted to defend her right, she would have to go to court.

"I must prove indisputably my claim to the land," she reflected, thinking rapidly. "But I must also be quick about it, or it will be too late to save the gold."

From the moment that Nancy had sighted the two aeroplanes, a daring plan had occurred to her. Glancing quickly over her shoulder to make sure that Sawtice and his companions did not see her, she crossed over to the nearest plane, and addressed the pilot.

"Did Mr Sawtice hire you to bring him here?"

"Yes, he did," the pilot returned crossly. "But he lied about the distance and beat me down on the price."

"Are you under contract to wait for him?"

"No. But of course I expected he'd want me to take him back. Why did you want to know?"

"Because I must get to Wellington Lake as soon as possible," Nancy replied. "These men are crooks and are trying to cheat me out of my property. I must get to the nearest telegraph station and wire my father. Will you take me and my friends?"

The pilot barely hesitated.

"Jump in, and we'll be off," he cried, opening the door of the cabin.

Nancy turned to bid Norman Ranny goodbye. To her surprise, he announced that he intended to accompany her.

"I've decided to go to Windham, Miss Drew. I've been thinking about it all day. Even if Annette has changed in her feelings towards me, I can't bear to leave her alone in a hospital."

"I'm glad you've changed your mind," Nancy said to him, her eyes shining.

It was not until the roar and crack of the engine had rent the air that the men who had taken possession of the land realized what was happening. With a shout of anger they ran towards the aircraft. The pilot turned his plane in a narrow space. Then, taxiing to the far end of the open stretch, he came roaring down the field.

Buck Sawtice and his fellow conspirators were hopelessly outdistanced. However, the pilot was so intent on avoiding them that he failed to see another man who had darted from the bushes, and was now running directly into the path of the oncoming plane.

"Stop! Stop!" he shouted, waving his arms.

# ·12·

## A Reunion

"It's Tom Stripe!" cried Nancy. "He'll be killed!"

The pilot swerved the plane barely in time to avoid disaster. It lifted from the ground, and rose sharply so as to miss by a fraction of an inch the pine trees that fringed the field.

"Whew!" Ranny ejaculated. "What a narrow escape!"

"Narrow for us, and narrow for Tom Stripe," Nancy declared, peering from the cabin window down at that scheming fellow on the ground. "I suspected he was party to a move to steal my land, and now I have definite proof of it."

"Do you suppose he's connected with the Yellow Dawn Mining Company?" George inquired thoughtfully.

"The company is in very poor repute up here in Canada," Ranny said. "It buys worthless land, issues shares in it, and sells the valueless shares to innocent buyers in the United States."

"I'd expect Tom Stripe to be involved in a scheme like that," Nancy returned.

She was eager to get to a telegraph office with the least possible delay, for she intended to wire her father in River Heights and tell him exactly what had happened. She felt certain that by getting in touch with the Velvet Company he would be able to establish her claim to the property.

Nancy thought of the old hollow oak near the Pierre Chap cabin. She had expected Norman Ranny to take her there the following day. Now that would be impossible.

"But I'll come back here within a week," she made up her mind. "Then I'll have a look at that famous old tree. Who knows! Perhaps I'll learn its secret!"

At Wellington Lake the party paused long enough for Nancy to communicate with Mrs Donnelly and to wire her father.

"I'll send word to Annette," Ranny decided, "and will tell her that as soon as I can possibly reach Windham I'll be with her. I can't get to her quickly enough. If in the meantime she should take a turn for the worse, I should never forgive myself for having hesitated."

"We'll all go there in the plane," Nancy offered. "Be ready in half an hour."

While the girls were busily occupied at Mrs Donnelly's boarding house, Ranny slipped away to a barber shop. At the appointed time he stood waiting for them at the landing field, but at first glance they failed to recognize him.

"Why, you've shaved off your beard," Bess gasped.

"You look years younger," George added admiringly.

During the journey from Wellington Lake to Windham, the girls could not refrain from stealing sly glances at Norman. They had never suspected that he was so handsome. Ranny scarcely spoke during the flight, but sat gazing out of the window.

The plane soon landed at a small airfield near Windham, and the party continued to the Good Hope Hospital by car. The prospector grew increasingly nervous.

"If anything has happened to Annette," he murmured, "I'll not be able to bear it."

Good news awaited the party on their arrival, however. Nancy was informed that the writer had been improving steadily ever since her operation.

"May I see her?" Ranny inquired eagerly.

The wire dispatched from Wellington Lake had prepared the novelist for the visit of her former sweetheart, and she was flushed and eager when he entered the room.

"Norman!" she exclaimed joyfully.

"Annette!" he cried, crossing towards her. "Can you ever forgive me?"

Nancy and her friends had waited in the corridor, but a few minutes later Annette and Norman insisted that they enter.

"I owe everything to you," the writer declared gratefully to Nancy. "As long as I live I'll never be able to thank you enough."

Everyone chatted excitedly for a few minutes, when a nurse presently came to warn the visitors that they must not stay too long. Once out in the corridor Ranny said soberly to Nancy:

"Annette and I know now that our separation was the result of an unfortunate circumstance. In some mysterious way the note she left for me in the hollow oak was exchanged for another. I'd give anything to learn who played that cruel trick on us."

"Perhaps we'll find out yet," Nancy told him.

Returning downstairs, an attendant handed the girl a telegram which had just been delivered.

"I'm sure it's from Dad," Nancy explained, tearing open the envelope. "I asked him to wire me at the hospital."

She read the lengthy message, the expression on her face denoting that its contents pleased her.

"Dad's coming here by plane," she announced. "He's as furious as I am about this scheme to steal my land."

"And he's making a special trip here to help you?" Bess asked.

"Not entirely. He also intends to look up some data on the Taylor lawsuit case while he's up north, so the trip will serve two purposes."

One of Norman Ranny's first missions during his stay in Windham was to visit his parents. Nancy and her chums agreed that after picking up Mr Drew at the airfield they should join the prospector at the farm.

The young people did not have long to wait, however, for the lawyer had chartered a plane very soon after his wire had been sent. Nancy ran over to greet him when he stepped from the plane.

"Oh, Dad, I'm so glad you're here," she cried. "I think it will take all your legal skill to save my property for me."

"That's quite likely," Mr Drew returned soberly. "Since I wired you I've had some more information."

"You mean bad news?"

"I'm afraid so, Nancy. Look at this message I received just as I took off from River Heights."

He produced a telegram from the Velvet Company.
It read:

CANNOT UNDERSTAND YOUR COMMUNICATION NANCY
DREW ASSIGNED ALL RIGHTS IN CONTEST PROPERTY TO
YELLOW DAWN MINING COMPANY FOR SMALL CONSIDERA-
TION.

Nancy's eyes flashed angrily as she returned the
telegram to her father.

"It's an outrage! I have not assigned my rights to any
company."

"You haven't signed your name to any papers?"
Carson Drew inquired anxiously.

"I've signed nothing."

"Then either your signature has been forged, or else
the Velvet Company is involved in this scheme to defraud you."

"It's straight robbery!"

"They haven't stolen the land yet," the lawyer told
her grimly. "I know we're up against a clever group of
schemers, but I think we will be able to find a way to
outwit them."

"I met one of the ringleaders," Nancy said. "I heard
him called Buck Sawtice."

Carson Drew nodded.

"He is the president of the so-called Yellow Dawn
Company. In actual fact he is the entire company, for
the rest of the men do his bidding. Tom Stripe is one of
his accomplices."

"I knew that, because he followed me to Wellington
Lake and tried to prevent me from returning here."

Carson Drew's face darkened.

"I was afraid he might make trouble for you. That

was one reason why I dropped everything and flew here to meet you."

"I'm glad you came," Nancy declared, putting her arms round him, "though I doubt even Tom Stripe would dare to attempt any violence."

"One can't be too sure, Nancy."

During the ride to the Ranny farmhouse Mr Drew listened to his daughter's account of everything that had taken place in Canada. When they heard the car drive up the lane, Mr and Mrs Ranny rushed out to greet Nancy and shower their thanks upon her for bringing their son home again.

"We were so worried after you took his picture with you," Mrs Ranny said, smiling. "We realize now how foolish we were. Norman has told us of your wonderful kindness to him."

Nancy and her friends were escorted into the house. After the first pleasantries had been exchanged, the conversation turned to more serious subjects, in which Carson Drew chanced to mention Buck Sawtice of the Yellow Dawn Mining Company.

A strange expression came into Mrs Ranny's eyes.

"Buck Sawtice!" she repeated.

"Yes. Do you know him?" the lawyer asked.

"He cost us our entire life savings," Mr Ranny said gruffly. "He and another man talked us into buying some worthless mining shares."

"We lost everything," his wife added. "We were forced to leave our home in Canada and come here. Now we work from morning until night, barely making enough to live on."

"I wish I had known about it," Norman said contritely. "I might have been able to help you."

"It wasn't your fault," his mother smiled fondly. "We couldn't tell you about our troubles, for we didn't know how to get in touch with you."

Carson Drew asked if he might see one of the shares of mining stock, and the owner obligingly found a certificate for him.

"May I keep it for a few days?" the lawyer requested. "It should be of help to me in my case against these men."

"Keep it as long as you like," the farmer said. "It's of no use to us. I can't understand why we have kept it all these years."

A few minutes later the girls took their leave of the Rannys. Norman accompanied his new friends to the waiting car.

"Will you be returning to Canada?" he asked Nancy.

"I'm not certain yet, though I believe that is the plan. Are you coming back with us?"

"That's what I wanted to talk to you about. As soon as Annette can be moved from the hospital, she is to be brought here."

"Oh, I'm so glad!" Nancy interrupted. "I know she'll improve rapidly under your mother's care."

"I feel sure she will, but she told me today she is greatly worried about Grandfather Pierre. I promised her I would return to Canada and search for him."

"Then of course you'll come back with us."

Carson Drew, who had overheard the conversation, now walked over to where they were standing.

"I think everyone is eager to reach Wellington Lake with the least possible delay. I believe we should fly there tonight. There's no time to lose."

# ·13·

## The Search

CARSON DREW's plan was to institute legal proceedings against the Yellow Dawn Mining Company. During the plane journey to Wellington Lake that night he confided to Nancy that he also suspected Tom Stripe and Buck Sawtice of being indirectly involved in the Marcus Taylor lumber case. He intended investigating the matter thoroughly before returning to River Heights.

"I never dreamed I'd get into so much trouble because I won the contest," Nancy remarked. "I thought the Velvet Company was an honest concern."

"I think it is. Naturally, the executives know nothing about you, so when they received the forged paper, which was doubtless the work of the Yellow Dawn officials, they more than likely never doubted its authenticity."

"That mistake may cost me my land. I shouldn't feel so bad about it if it were an ordinary piece of property, but now that it seems as if gold may be found there I can't bear the thought of losing it."

"We'll fight for your rights to the bitter end," her father assured her. "I feel partly responsible for all the trouble. If I had recorded your deed immediately after you received it, your position would have been far more secure."

"It wasn't your fault, Dad. We knew nothing about the ground. If it had turned out to be worthless I would probably have refused to accept it from the Velvet Company."

"We are up against a clever, unscrupulous group of men, and it will take all our ingenuity to combat them," concluded Carson Drew soberly.

Some minutes later the plane make a skilful landing at Wellington Lake, not far from Mrs Donnelly's boarding house. Although it was late, a light still gleamed in a window.

"She'll be surprised to see us return so soon," Nancy chuckled.

Mrs Donnelly was locking up for the night when the little party arrived. Learning that they had left Windham without having had their evening meal, she insisted on preparing a light snack for them before they went to bed. Over their cups of cocoa, Mrs Donnelly listened to Nancy's account of the plot to deprive her of the property.

"The Yellow Dawn Mining Company!" the woman exclaimed, upon hearing the name.

"Yes. Have you ever heard of it?" Nancy asked eagerly.

"Under most unpleasant circumstances. I once bought some mining shares from that concern. I should have known better, for I'm not easily taken in on business deals."

"Was the stock sold to you by a man named Buck Sawtice?" Mr Drew queried.

"No! I'd never buy anything from that fellow!"

"What can you tell me about him?" the lawyer asked quickly.

"I know him only by reputation, Mr Drew. However, he is a partner in a lumber company which I suspect of being dishonest."

"I was hoping that I might uncover just such information," the lawyer returned, highly pleased. "I will follow up the clue you have just given me."

"I'm sorry I can't tell you any of the details," Mrs Donnelly said regretfully, "though I can refer you to a man who might give you more information."

She wrote out the name of a local lawyer and gave the paper to Carson Drew, who promised to call on him as soon as possible.

It was after midnight before the lights were turned out, and everyone went to bed. At seven o'clock the following morning Nancy came downstairs to find that her father had risen before her.

"Mr Drew went down to the village," Mrs Donnelly told her, "but said he expected to be back here in time for breakfast."

However, when an hour and a half had elapsed and still her father had not returned, Nancy grew troubled.

"If he doesn't get here soon it will ruin all our plans for the day," she declared.

At that moment Carson Drew was sighted coming up the path, walking briskly. His face wore an animated expression.

"Good news, Father?" Nancy asked.

"Yes. I have definite evidence that Sawtice is tied up in a scheme to rob Marcus Taylor of his lumber interests here in the north," he told her, sitting down to a hearty breakfast which Mrs Donnelly had kept warm for him. "I think I've gathered enough material this morning to win the case."

"I'm glad of that," Nancy said. "If we could only recover my mining property everything ought to turn out splendidly."

"I'll visit your land today, if I can arrange it, and have a talk with Sawtice if he is working there," Carson Drew announced.

Norman Ranny, who was sitting nearby, overheard the remark.

"It can be easily arranged, Mr Drew. I know this country as well as any guide. I have a boat here at Wellington Lake, and will be only too glad to take you with me."

"It doesn't seem fair to put you to so much trouble. If you will accept payment——"

"I couldn't, Mr Drew. Your daughter has done me a service I shall never be able to repay. Besides, I am eager to return to Mr Chap's cabin on my own account."

"Then we'll accept your offer gratefully, Mr Ranny. How soon can we start?"

"In fifteen minutes, if you like."

"I'll be ready," Mr Drew promised.

"And so will we," Nancy added, speaking for her friends.

The girls hurried to their rooms to put on more suitable clothes. By the time Norman Ranny had the boat and camping equipment ready the group was waiting for him at the pier.

The prospector chose a route similar to the one Pete Atkins had previously taken. The party rowed across Wellington Lake, and then struck out again along the shore of Stewart Lake. Mr Drew and Norman Ranny took turns at rowing. Since time was precious, a lunch Mrs Donnelly had packed was eaten en route.

"We've made good time," the prospector declared after a time, squinting up at the sun. "That's the Chap cabin over yonder."

Far across the lake the girls caught a glimpse of the log structure. Nancy was quick to observe that no smoke was curling from the chimney.

"I hope we find Mr Chap this time," she said, looking troubled. "You don't suppose he has had an accident, do you?"

"It isn't like Mr Chap to be away for days at a time," Norman Ranny commented. "I'm beginning to feel worried about him."

With the goal so near, the prospector bent to his oars with a will. Ten minutes later the boat grated on the sandy beach.

While the guide and Mr Drew dragged the craft from the water, Nancy, George and Bess ran on ahead to find out if Mr Chap were at home. As Nancy came into the clearing, she halted abruptly. The cabin had been boarded up!

"Well, of all things!" she exclaimed in astonishment. "What in the world does this mean?"

Bess and George were equally bewildered. They ran back to the beach to tell the men the news, and they came at once to see for themselves.

"I can't understand it," the prospector said, gloomily examining the covered windows and door. "It looks as if Grandfather Chap may have returned here yesterday and closed up the place himself. As far as I know, he expected to remain here for the summer."

"His crops are planted," Nancy observed. "And the cupboards inside the house are filled with groceries."

"I don't like the look of things," Ranny confessed.

"Do you think he has met with foul play?" Nancy asked quickly.

"I don't know what to think. Tom Stripe and Raymond Niles acted suspiciously, to say the least. They tied me up and left me. If Grandfather Chap happened to have been in their way, they would have treated him the same way."

"Would it be possible to break into the house and make certain that he isn't a prisoner inside?" Nancy asked.

"I think I can pry off one of the boards over the rear window," Ranny decided, making an inspection.

After considerable trouble the prospector succeeded in removing the barrier. While Nancy and her companions waited outside, he climbed through the window and disappeared inside. Shortly afterwards he returned.

"Everything is just exactly as we left it," he reported. "Mr Chap isn't here."

He carefully boarded up the window again.

"I suppose there's nothing to do but to continue on our journey," Nancy said in disappointment. "It begins to look as if Mr Chap really has left the place for good."

Gloomily the party returned to the beach. While the girls took care of the oars and light equipment, Carson Drew and Norman Ranny carried the boat a short distance to the rushing stream, which ran deeper into the woods. After an uneventful journey the craft was finally drawn up near the Dawson cabin.

"How is Pete?" Nancy questioned anxiously, after she had greeted Mrs Dawson.

"Greatly improved," the woman assured her. "This morning he ate a hearty meal and walked about for a few minutes. Of course, he's still very weak. He and

Jake went out to the barn a few minutes ago. I'll call them."

There was no need for her to do so, however. As she went over to the door Mrs Dawson saw her elder son hurrying towards the house.

"I tried to stop him but I couldn't!" he exclaimed, when he was within earshot. "There's no telling what he may do!"

"Jake, what are you talking about?" his mother demanded.

"Pete Atkins!" the boy explained. "He said he's going to run down Tom Stripe and square things up!"

# ·14·

## Mr Drew's Strategy

It was too late to overtake the guide. Pete Atkins had slipped away into the dense woods, avoiding the well-worn trails.

"What a pity he didn't wait," Mr Drew said regretfully. "Soon the police will be here."

This was news to the others, since the lawyer had not mentioned that he had called on the sheriff that morning in Wellington Lake. There he had been assured that men would be sent immediately to protect Nancy's property.

"An expert surveyor will come along, too," Mr Drew told his daughter. "After he has gone over the land we'll know exactly where we stand. Until we are absolutely certain that the property is the same as that deeded to you by the Velvet Company, we shall have to move slowly."

"How many men will the sheriff bring with him?" Norman Ranny inquired.

"Not very many, I am afraid. It would be a good idea if we could round up some others. Buck Sawtice and his men are likely to offer us armed resistance."

"I think we could find a number of woodsmen who might be willing to join the posse," the prospector said.

"I'll be glad to go," Mr Dawson spoke up. "And both of my sons are mighty handy when it comes to protectin' property."

"We hope there will be no necessity for a fight," Mr Drew returned, "though we shall have to be prepared for it."

Norman Ranny knew of several families living in the area. While he rode in one direction to spread word of the gathering posse, Nancy and George with young Jake went the opposite way to ask for similar help. They returned to the Dawson cabin with several neighbours riding behind them.

During their absence the Wellington Lake sheriff and his deputies had arrived, and the yard swarmed with horsemen. A few minutes later Norman Ranny returned with more men.

As the group waited for orders to start off, Mr Drew crossed over to where the girls were standing with Mrs Dawson. Nancy knew at once what he was going to say.

"Now, Dad, don't tell us we can't go," she forestalled him. "With all these men along to protect us, you surely can't say it won't be safe."

"That's just what I intended to say, you young rascal!"

"We'll be very careful, if you let us go along."

"The trip will be a dangerous one, Nancy. I'll not be able to keep an eye on all of you. If there were only some way we could keep in close communication with one another, even though separated——"

"I know a way!" Nancy cried, her eyes lighting up.

"How?" Mr Drew smiled.

"Why, the old hollow oak tree!"

"I don't understand."

"You couldn't, because I've never told you about it. On the Chap property there is an old hollow oak tree which would be an ideal place to leave a message. I propose that if any one of us gets into trouble, that person will try to drop a note in the tree."

It was obvious, however, that Carson Drew was not particularly impressed with the idea.

"I've never even seen this tree," he protested.

"Mr Ranny can point it out so that everyone will know where it is," Nancy went on, growing more enthusiastic as she spoke. "He told me only a few minutes ago that we would pass close to it on our way to my property."

Mr Drew conceded defeat.

"If I turn this idea down, I feel sure you'll think up another," he laughed. "I'm still convinced that it is unwise to take you with me, though I suppose I must give in."

"How can we leave any notes without paper or pencil?" Bess asked doubtfully.

Nancy ran to the house for the necessary articles, which she distributed among her friends.

"I know you think the plan won't work," she told her father a little later as he helped her into the saddle, "but you never can tell."

"Perhaps it isn't as wild a scheme as I thought at first, Nancy. At least I'll reserve judgment until after I've seen this mysterious old oak."

The posse set off through the trees, and slowly began the steep, rocky ascent. As she rounded a bend in the trail, Nancy suddenly reined her horse to a halt, for through the trees she had caught a glimpse of a dark shape lying prone on the ground. She was almost certain it was a man. Waiting motionless, she watched the figure in the bushes in case it was an ambush. It did not move.

Nancy sprang from the saddle and, tossing the reins over a small bush, she pushed aside the foliage. There she came upon Pete Atkins, lying face downwards on the ground.

"Pete!" she cried fearfully.

The guide made no response as the girl attempted to turn him over. Then she noticed that his shirt was saturated with blood. Alarmed, Nancy ran back, calling for help.

"Come quickly, Father!" she cried.

All the riders urged their horses on to a faster pace. Upon reaching the bend in the trail, they hastily dismounted.

"Careful, men," the sheriff warned them. "This may be a trick."

On the alert for any trouble, the men followed Nancy to the place where Pete Atkins lay.

"Pete's been shot. Comb the woods and see if you can find the person who did it!" the sheriff ordered, bending down to examine the guide.

He had brought along a first-aid kit, and after probing about for the bullet, bandaged the wounded shoulder. As the officer worked, the guide opened his eyes and groaned with pain.

"Who did it, Pete?" the sheriff asked gently.

The man was too exhausted to answer him.

"It must have been an unprovoked attack," Norman Ranny announced furiously. "I imagine Pete was shot from behind!"

*Quickly Nancy ran to help the wounded man.*

The members of the posse were returning from their unsuccessful search of the surrounding woods. No one had been sighted.

"Will Pete be all right?" Nancy asked the sheriff anxiously.

"Yes, I think his chances are very good," she was told. "But he's so weak from loss of blood that we won't be able to take him with us."

"Can you assign one of the men to remain with him?"

"That's probably the best thing to do," the sheriff agreed.

One of the men from Wellington Lake was selected for that duty. Pete was moved carefully to a more comfortable place and they all prepared to move on again.

As the party continued grimly along the trail at a much swifter pace than before, Carson Drew, anxious for their safety, rode close to the girls. At length the posse arrived at the knoll from which Nancy had previously viewed her property. Here the riders halted.

Nancy, her father and Norman Ranny all dismounted. In the valley below they could see several men working feverishly near the cliff where Ranny had discovered gold.

"There's Buck Sawtice directing the removal of the ore," the prospector announced bitterly, training his powerful binoculars on one of the men.

He handed the glasses to Nancy.

"I take it that Sawtice will refuse to allow our man to survey the property," Carson Drew remarked, thinking aloud.

"That's to be expected," the prospector agreed. "He'll not give up the land if he can help it."

"No. But if we take the camp by surprise, the chance of their resisting will be much less."

"We can descend from the knoll without being seen from below," Ranny stated. "The tall bushes make a perfect screen."

So saying, he indicated a trail Nancy had not seen during her previous visit. The two men returned to the sheriff to give their orders.

Nancy was about to follow, when a slight sound in the bushes attracted her attention. She saw a man crawling rapidly on his hands and knees through the foliage. Then he scrambled to his feet and raced madly towards the camp below.

"A lookout!" Nancy called in frantic warning. "Stop him before he gives the alarm!"

# ·15·

## Startling Information

It was too late to overtake the lookout, for he had dashed far down the steep slope. Carson Drew ordered the posse to gallop down to the camp, for he saw there was no further advantage to be gained by cautious manœuvres.

Nancy sprang into the saddle. With her friends riding beside her, she followed the posse into the valley.

Buck Sawtice had been warned of the approach, but realized that since his men were outnumbered, it would be useless to resist. So, unexpectedly, Carson Drew was greeted with a show of civility. The lawyer adopted a similar conciliatory attitude.

"There's been a good deal of misunderstanding about this property," Mr Drew began. "According to a deed which my daughter holds, this land belongs to her."

Sawtice tried to look surprised.

"It cannot belong to your daughter, for I hold the title to it. I have received a deed from the Velvet Company."

"Have you the paper with you?" Carson Drew queried.

"Well, no, I haven't."

"Then I'm sure you'll have no objection to our surveyor staking out my daughter's plot. Before we make any claim to this property we must be absolutely certain we are right."

Buck Sawtice obviously objected to such a proposal, and seemed to be on the verge of angrily refusing the request, when his eyes wandered to the grim line of men who stood directly behind the lawyer. Then he changed his mind.

"I should be very glad to have you survey the land," he said coldly. "I feel sure that it will help in proving my right to the property."

While the surveyor and his helpers were setting up their equipment, Nancy wandered aimlessly about the land. She was disturbed to see that Sawtice and his men had begun to blast into the cliff where Ranny had discovered gold.

She bent down to examine an oddly-coloured piece of rock. Convinced that it contained streaks of gold, she slipped it into her pocket, intending to ask Mr Ranny's opinion about it later.

Suddenly she heard the sound of a conversation being carried on in low tones. The speakers were screened from view by bushes and rocks, but Nancy crept closer, suspecting that they might perhaps be Sawtice's men. Even at such a close range the conversation was unintelligible.

Suddenly it dawned on her that the two men were speaking French. She had studied the language at school, but this conversation moved so rapidly that it was difficult for her to catch all that was being said.

"I can jot down the words now and translate them later," she told herself, drawing a pencil and pad from her pocket. "It will be much easier when I see them written out."

She managed to catch several phrases, which appeared formidable to her as she wrote them on paper.

Suddenly somebody tapped her on the shoulder. Nancy stifled a scream as she wheeled round to face Tom Stripe.

"You! Here!" she gasped.

The man was glancing at the notebook, trying to make out what she had written.

"Don't look so startled," he smirked. "What are you writing, anyway?"

Relieved, Nancy realized that the man could not read French.

"I always carry a notebook with me," she evaded neatly. "I like to jot down my impressions of scenery and people."

This answer seemed to satisfy Stripe. However, his tone became slightly menacing as he said, "This isn't a very safe place for you to be taking notes."

"It's my land, Tom Stripe!"

"It *was* your land, you mean," he sneered. "I gave you a chance to sell and you wouldn't take it. Now it's too late."

"That remains to be seen. If I lose the property, I'll always be glad that I refused to have business dealings with a man like you!"

Tom Stripe moved closer, and for a second Nancy thought he was going to strike her. But her significant glance towards the surveyor, who was working not far away, seemed to warn him not to do anything. With an angry gesture he turned and walked away.

Nancy raced back to find her father or Mr Ranny, but they were nowhere to be seen.. Bess and George, who were sitting on a boulder watching the surveyor, greeted her eagerly.

"Where have you been, Nancy?" Bess asked. "We were beginning to grow alarmed, for George thought she saw Tom Stripe skulking round here."

"You were quite right," Nancy said to George. "I met him just a minute ago."

"Did he try to harm you?" George queried anxiously.

"I think he would have liked to, but there were too many people around. It certainly was lucky for me that he never learned French."

"What are you talking about, Nancy?" Bess asked in bewilderment.

In answer, Nancy laughingly took the notebook from her pocket. Her face grew unusually serious as she read what she had copied.

" 'Old recluse has been sent by new owner here on wild chase. Meanwhile, men are robbing fellow of his property—say he will never come back alive.' "

"How dreadful!" Bess exclaimed, as she peered over Nancy's shoulder.

"I'm not surprised that it almost frightened you to death when Tom Stripe tried to translate your notes," George added. "Oh, do you suppose Mr Chap really has been harmed?"

"He has been tricked, and his life is in danger. The men said a great deal more, but they talked so rapidly I couldn't catch everything."

"What can we do to save poor Mr Chap?" Bess asked, greatly worried.

"I'm going to tell Mr Ranny and Dad," Nancy declared. "They may decide to organize a search party."

George glared at Buck Sawtice, who was working a short distance away.

"I'll bet *he* could tell where Mr Chap has gone," she said furiously. "I'd like to walk over there and accuse him."

She rose from the rock with the idea of carrying out this intention, when Nancy caught her by the arm.

"Don't do anything rash, George. We mustn't let anyone suspect what we know. If we do, we will lose all chance of finding Mr Chap."

"I suppose you're right, Nancy. I know I am inclined to be too hot-headed."

"There's Mr Ranny now," Bess indicated.

"I'll go over and talk to him," Nancy said hastily.

She drew the prospector aside and showed him the notebook. His face grew stern as he read the words written in French.

"Tom Stripe and Buck Sawtice are behind all this!" he cried angrily. "I'll have it out with them right away and learn the truth."

"That's what George wanted to do," Nancy smiled. "But I believe that's not the best way. We haven't enough evidence to accuse anyone yet. I thought that if you would scout around and follow Stripe and his friends, we might perhaps find Mr Chap and at the same time get proof of his abduction."

At these words Norman Ranny smothered his anger, for he realized that Nancy's suggestion was a wise one. After he had warned the girl to destroy her notes in case they should fall into the hands of someone who could read them, he moved swiftly away.

Nancy did not have a chance until some time later to tell her father what she had overheard. When he joined her after a lengthy talk with the surveyor, he too had news to report.

"I'm making excellent progress in gathering data to be used in the Taylor lumber case," Carson Drew declared enthusiastically. "The surveyor gave me a few tips which I mean to investigate as soon as I return to Wellington Lake."

"I'm glad of that," his daughter replied. "We'll clear up two problems with one trip."

"Of course we can't do much here until after the survey has been made."

"I realize that, Dad; in fact, I've not given much thought to my property rights since we arrived here. I've been too worried about Mr Chap."

"No doubt he's just away on holiday somewhere, Nancy."

"That's what I thought when we saw his cabin all boarded up, but I know now he can't be. I have evidence that Sawtice kidnapped Pierre Chap in order to steal his property."

She produced her notes. After Mr Drew had read them carefully Nancy tore them into tiny bits which she scattered to the winds.

"What do you think about this, Dad?" she queried.

"It looks as if you have uncovered a real clue, Nancy. Of course, what you overheard may have been mere, idle gossip."

"I realize that, but even if the evidence doesn't bear weight in court, it serves as something to work on. I've asked Norman Ranny to do a little scouting before we openly accuse Sawtice."

"You've handled the matter very well," Mr Drew praised her. "If nothing develops within the next few hours I shall organize search parties and comb the woods for Mr Chap."

In spite of her father's words, Nancy did not feel that she was doing much to help find Pierre Chap. The longer she thought about it the more worried she became. She feared that even a few hours delay might mean the difference between life and death.

She glanced anxiously round the camp for Norman Ranny, but the prospector had disappeared. Thinking that he might still be at the place where the horses had been tethered, the girl ran over to look. As luck would have it, the prospector was just then riding away.

"Mr Ranny!" she called frantically.

The man heard her, and turned his horse round.

"Take me with you," Nancy pleaded.

"But it won't be safe for you where I'm going," he protested.

"Oh, but I've changed my mind about wanting you to look for Mr Chap," she told him breathlessly. "Instead, I want you to take me to the hollow oak!"

"The hollow oak!"

Nancy was busy untying her horse.

"Yes. I've just had a hunch. I think it may contain a valuable clue to what has become of Pierre Chap!"

# • 16 •

## The Hidden Chest

If NORMAN RANNY had any doubts about a journey to the famous old "letter box" oak, he kept them to himself. So he and Nancy rode over the narrow trail in silence, until finally they came near a waterfall.

"This is the northern edge of Pierre Chap's land," the prospector explained as he led the way through an avenue of stately trees. Soon they approached a giant gnarled oak which stood by itself in a tiny clearing.

The prospector indicated a dead limb which had split from the trunk.

"That's the bough that almost finished me."

Nancy crossed over to the ancient tree.

"Mr Ranny, please tell me where the hollow 'letter box' is," she eagerly said to her companion.

Ranny showed her a cleverly concealed cavity far up the trunk at a point where two of the boughs came together. It was nearly out of reach for Nancy, so she stood up on tiptoe to peer into it.

"It seems to extend far back into the tree."

"Yes," the prospector agreed. "At one time a swarm of bees decided to adopt that hollow, and until we could get rid of them Annette and I thought we'd lose our letter box."

Nancy thrust her hand into the opening, but brought it out empty.

"It looks as if my hunch wasn't such a good one, Mr Ranny."

"What did you expect to find?"

"I don't know," Nancy admitted. "Something just seemed to tell me to come to this old oak. I had a feeling that I might find a communication of some kind about Mr Chap."

"That's highly unlikely."

"I suppose I have brought you here on a wild chance," Nancy said apologetically. "But now that we've made the trip, I guess I may as well examine the hollow carefully. Would you please lift me up, Mr Ranny, so that I can run my hand into the back of the cavity?"

Obligingly he lifted her, and Nancy once more thrust her arm into the opening.

"I can feel something!" the girl announced excitedly. "It rustles just like paper!"

"It's probably a dead leaf."

"No, it's a piece of paper," Nancy maintained. "But it's just beyond my reach."

"Let me go after it," the prospector urged, beginning to share in her enthusiasm.

Nancy made way for him, but the paper was too far down in the hollow even for his grasp.

"Wait. I'll get a stick," the girl cried.

She found one with a knob on the end. Ranny held her up again. This time she was successful in raking in the paper. Triumphantly she held it up to the light.

"It's a message! It is!" she cried.

"Read it," Ranny commanded tensely.

It was difficult for Nancy to keep her voice steady as she began:

*"Fearing for my life at the hands of Buck Sawtice and his gang, I am placing this message in the hollow oak, trusting that if anything should happen to me it will some day be found.*

*"I hope that the one who discovers this letter will be you, Annette, my granddaughter, who married the Ranny boy against my will. I realize now that my attitude was misguided, and I beg your forgiveness for having attempted to prevent your wedding.*

*"I have hidden my money at the base of this tree. The inheritance is yours, Annette. Keep it with my blessing, and try to forgive your loving grandfather.*

*Pierre Chap."*

"Let me read it for myself!" Norman Ranny cried as Nancy finished. "I surely can't have heard correctly. Is it possible that Grandfather Pierre believed that Annette and I were married?"

"It appears that he did," Nancy replied, handing him the note for his inspection. "What does he mean by the reference to his money? Do you suppose he actually hid a treasure here beside the tree?"

"Grandfather Pierre never had a great deal of confidence in banks. He hoarded funds which he kept in the house."

"Then the treasure must be buried here, as he states. If we only had something with which to dig!"

"I'll go back and get a spade. It won't take long. You're not afraid to stay here alone, are you, Miss Drew?"

"No," Nancy said staunchly. "Only try to hurry as fast as you can, and be careful that no one follows you back here."

"I'll be back in fifteen minutes if luck is with me," the prospector promised.

When she was left alone in the still, deep woods, Nancy occupied her time trying to determine the exact spot where the treasure might be buried, and soon found a patch of recently turned earth.

"This must be where the money is hidden," she said to herself. "Oh, I wish Mr Ranny would hurry!"

She sat down, her back against the gnarled tree, and waited. Fifteen minutes passed. Then ten more. Still nothing to break the deep silence!

Suddenly there came the clatter of hoofs along the trail, and Nancy jumped up quickly. Not until Norman Ranny appeared did she relax.

"Did I frighten you?" the prospector asked.

"A little," Nancy admitted. "I wasn't sure that it was you."

She then showed him the patch of loose earth and he began to dig. Presently his spade struck something hard.

"There's something here, all right!" he declared tensely.

Turning over a little more of the earth, he uncovered a metal chest. Lifting it from the ground, he handed it over to Nancy to open.

With trembling fingers the girl unfastened the clasp, and the lid fell back. Within the chest there lay stack upon stack of notes, as well as some loose ones and a number of gold coins.

As Nancy and Ranny peered down at the treasure, dazed by the discovery, a sudden wind caught up a few of the notes and scattered them on the grass. Nancy slammed down the lid of the chest, and the two darted about, picking up the scattered money.

"I guess we have it all," she said at length, returning the loose notes to the container.

"What shall we do with the chest?" Ranny asked with a worried frown. "We dare not take it back to camp."

"I suppose the safest thing will be to bury it again."

"But not in the same hole."

They looked about the clearing for a suitable hiding place. Nancy finally found one near a sandstone boulder. Ranny dug a new hole, and with a careful glance in all directions to make certain that no one was watching, the two placed the chest in it.

Then, while Nancy tramped down the loose dirt over the chest and scattered dry leaves to conceal their work, the prospector carefully refilled the first gap in the earth beneath the old oak, and smoothed down the surface dirt.

"There, that's the very best we can do," he announced, picking up his spade. "We may as well get away from here."

"The sooner the better," Nancy agreed.

They mounted their horses and rode rapidly towards the camp. They both avoided speaking of Pierre Chap. The discovery of the note he had left in the hollow tree had chilled their hearts with the fear that the old man might be dead.

"Buck Sawtice holds the clue to his fate," Nancy thought. "If I only knew of some way in which to force that man to reveal the truth!"

They were now drawing near the mining camp. Nancy suddenly glanced down at her wrist, and noticed that a gold bracelet she had been wearing was missing. At her cry of alarm Ranny halted his pony to inquire what was wrong.

"I've lost my bracelet! It must have fallen from my

wrist when I was sitting by the oak tree. I remember unclasping it. If anyone should find it near the place where the treasure is hidden, he might grow suspicious as to why we were there. It had my name inside."

"We'd better ride back for it."

"I don't so much mind losing the bracelet, even though it is a good one," Nancy said apologetically as they turned their horses, "but I am afraid it would reveal a clue to the finder, something I don't want known just now."

"Especially if it should come into the hands of one of Buck Sawtice's men," Ranny added. "They doubtless know Grandfather Pierre hid his money somewhere near here and are trying to force him to reveal the hiding place."

Within a few minutes they drew near the hollow oak and tied their horses in a clump of bushes some distance away. As they walked along the path, Nancy caught sight of fresh footprints in the moist earth, footprints which did not in the least resemble Ranny's. She called her companion's attention to them.

Stooping to examine them, he declared, "Someone has passed by this way since we left here a few minutes ago."

They proceeded at a more cautious pace. As they drew near the clearing they halted, and peered through the bushes.

Nancy started. She saw a man examining the soft earth near the base of the hollow oak. It was none other than Tom Stripe!

"He must have followed me from camp when I went for the spade," Ranny whispered.

"Do you think he saw us dig up the treasure?"

"I doubt it. He seems a little suspicious of the loose earth, but doesn't quite know what to make of it."

"I hope we gathered up all the banknotes that blew away," Nancy whispered nervously. "If he were to find one of those he'd be almost certain to suspect the truth."

As she spoke, they heard Tom Stripe utter a low exclamation of surprise. He reached down and picked up an object from the loose dirt.

"He has found my bracelet!" Nancy gasped.

# ·17·

## The Lost Bracelet

"He has found my bracelet!" Nancy repeated, as she recognized the object Tom Stripe had picked up from the soft earth.

The man did not seem to know what to make of the discovery, for he turned the trinket over and over in his hand, finally placing it in his pocket. Glancing carefully about him, he walked over to a clump of bushes not far from the place where Nancy and Norman Ranny were hiding, and picked up a spade. As he walked back to the old oak he began to dig the loose earth at its base.

Nancy watched him, fascinated. How had he known that the treasure chest had been hidden beneath the oak? She was convinced that he had not guessed the truth, and that the bracelet had not been the clue. He had brought his spade to the site on purpose to look for the buried money.

Tensely the two waited. Would Tom Stripe find the new hiding place after discovering the hole was empty? He was already a bit suspicious. They could hear him muttering under his breath as he rested.

"This must be the place," Nancy caught the words. "It fits old Chap's description. Looks like someone has beat me here."

Convinced that Stripe had known about the hidden

chest, Nancy whispered a plan to her companion. Ranny nodded that he understood, and crept back to the place where the horses had been left. He returned a moment later, bringing with him a long coil of rope.

"Do you think you can lasso him from this distance?" Nancy whispered anxiously.

Ranny did not reply. Instead, he stepped out into the open, his rope swinging. It swished swiftly through the air, and settled neatly over Tom Stripe's shoulders.

Taken completely by surprise, the man dropped his spade and uttered a terrified yell. As he struggled to free himself, Ranny drew the rope taut about his captive's waist.

"Let me go!" the prisoner snarled.

"All in good time," Nancy replied pleasantly. "Tie him to the tree, Mr Ranny."

Tom Stripe made a desperate effort to free himself, but was unable to move. The prospector then trussed him securely to the trunk of the old oak.

"What do you want?" the prisoner demanded. "If it's the money, I haven't got it."

"So we noticed," Nancy responded. "You may as well tell us the truth, Tom Stripe. Who told you about Mr Chap's money?"

The prisoner maintained a sullen silence.

"What have you done with Mr Chap?" Nancy demanded sharply.

The only answer was a sardonic smile.

Ranny tried next. Though he threatened the man, he could not get a word from him. Realizing that such tactics were useless, Nancy drew Ranny aside for a consultation.

"What will we do?" the girl asked. "We must make

him talk, for I feel certain he can tell us where Grand-father Pierre is."

"I think I can make him tell the truth," Ranny returned grimly. "I'll not hurt him, but I intend to give him a good scare. Whatever I do, back me up. Don't lose your nerve. I think he'll talk!"

Nancy was almost as troubled as the prisoner when the prospector began to gather together a pile of dry sticks which he placed at the base of the oak tree.

Then he drew a match from his pocket. Stripe watched with terrified eyes as the prospector lit the dry wood. A tiny flame leaped up, licking at the prisoner's boots.

It was all Nancy could do to keep from pleading with Ranny to extinguish the blaze. Yet she recalled his promise that he would not harm the man.

"Now will you talk?" Ranny asked.

Tom Stripe moistened his lips. He gazed down at the fire. The last shred of his courage vanished.

"Put out the fire! Put it out!" he screamed. "I'll tell you the truth!"

Nancy darted forward to help Ranny stamp out the flames. The prisoner had not been hurt, though he was almost hysterical with fright.

"All right. Out with the story," the prospector ordered.

"I knew all about the hidden chest," Stripe gasped. "I tortured Pierre Chap and forced him to tell me where he had hidden it."

Ranny involuntarily stepped forward as if to strike the prisoner, but with an effort he controlled his temper.

"Where is Mr Chap now?" Nancy questioned, after Stripe had finished.

The captive hesitated, then said:

"He's hidden in an old cave about six miles from here. It's called Gordon's Grotto."

"I know where you mean," Ranny nodded.

"You stay here and watch Stripe," Nancy suggested. "I'll race back to camp and tell the sheriff. The posse can start for Gordon's Grotto in a few minutes."

The prospector wrote out complete directions for reaching the cave, and with these safe in her pocket, Nancy galloped back to the mining camp. She was soon there, and as she dismounted a man came to meet her. With a start she recognized Raymond Niles.

"So you're here, too!"

"Oh, I've been close by all the time," the man smiled disarmingly. "But I've taken no part in this scheme to defraud you of your land."

"Oh, no!" Nancy retorted sarcastically.

"It's the truth. I did try to buy your property, but I have a great distaste for the whole affair now. Since I've met you and found you such a charming young lady——"

"I don't care for your admiration, Mr Niles! Let me pass."

With a toss of her head Nancy moved past him and went to find the sheriff. She quickly informed him of all that had happened near the hollow oak.

"I'll send some of my deputies there now to take Stripe prisoner," the man promised. "I'll dispatch another group to Gordon's Grotto."

At Nancy's suggestion, great care was taken to prevent Buck Sawtice from suspecting what was going on. But when the two groups of men rode away from the camp he strode angrily over to Carson Drew.

"What are you up to now?" he demanded.

"I'm sure I don't know what you mean," the lawyer retorted.

"You know well enough! But I'm tired of all this trouble. I'm willing to make your daughter a fair offer for her land!"

Carson Drew could not restrain a smile. He had seen Sawtice talking with the surveyor earlier, and surmised that the latter had refused to be bribed or intimidated.

"What do you consider a fair price, Mr Sawtice?"

"A thousand dollars."

"That's not very much for property that contains gold," Mr Drew smiled.

"It's my best offer. If you don't take it I may not be so generous again." So saying, Sawtice turned and walked away.

Carson Drew sought his daughter to tell her the latest development. As they were discussing it the surveyor joined them.

"I've practically finished my work," he announced.

"And is the land mine?" Nancy questioned eagerly.

"Absolutely. However, it's my own opinion someone is going to be badly disappointed about this property."

"What do you mean?" Mr Drew asked.

The surveyor lowered his voice.

"It happens I know a little about mining. After going over this property today I'm inclined to doubt that the veins of gold are very extensive. In my opinion it would cost more to mine the ore than it would ever be worth."

"Sawtice has offered my daughter a thousand dollars for it."

"I'd take it," the surveyor advised. "The land is of no use for farming."

"What do you think, Nancy?" her father asked.

"I scarcely know what to say, Dad. I think I'll not make my decision quite yet."

Nancy was disappointed. At first she had never dared hope that gold would be found on her land, but the events of the past few days had led her to think otherwise.

"We can't stay here in the woods indefinitely," Mr Drew told his daughter gently. "After all, the land cost you nothing, and you came here to inspect it, anticipating a possible disappointment."

"I suppose it would be best to sell, only——"

"Many a dollar has been lost because the trader held on, hoping that the market would turn."

"You're right. I'll sell. When you see Sawtice tell him I accept his offer. Only I dislike having dealings with a man like that."

"If it turns out that he harmed Pierre Chap in any way, there'll be another reckoning with him," the lawyer promised.

He went to find Sawtice, and the two conferred together for some time. Nancy joined them at her father's call.

"Mr Sawtice has agreed to pay cash for the land," he told her. "He will send a plane to the city for it immediately. As soon as the money arrives, you are to sign over the land, and we'll start for home. Is that plan satisfactory?"

"Perfectly," Nancy declared. "Mr Sawtice, would you object if I asked your pilot to carry a message for me to the States?"

The man frowned, but said gruffly, "It's entirely up to him. If he wants to carry a letter, it's nothing to me."

Before Nancy could write out a note to Annette Chapelle asking her to come north if she were able to do so, she saw Buck Sawtice talking to the pilot.

"I wonder if he's telling him not to take the letter," she thought.

A few minutes later when she made her request to the pilot, he seemed reluctant to help her.

"I don't see how I can take the note, Miss. I'll not have time to deliver it, let alone post it anywhere."

Raymond Niles, who was standing nearby, had overheard the conversation. Determined to make a favourable impression on Nancy, he stepped forward.

"Go ahead and take the letter," he told the pilot. "I'll be responsible to Sawtice."

"All right," the pilot agreed. "Give it to me."

Nancy handed him the message with instructions for its delivery, and a little later the plane took off.

The girl was glad that Raymond Niles had helped her, though she did not feel especially grateful to him, for she was well aware of his purpose. She disliked the man intensely.

"Don't rush away," he coaxed her, as she turned after watching the take-off.

"I can't stop and talk now," she told him hurriedly.

She had caught a glimpse of the sheriff's posse returning from the search for Pierre Chap, and ran to meet the riders.

## · 18 ·

## *Treachery*

THEY regarded her coldly. Aware that something was wrong, Nancy sought the sheriff, who spoke to her in terse sentences.

"It was nothing but a hoax. We had a hard ride, only to find that no one had been imprisoned in the cave. Most likely Chap's safe in his cabin now."

"Tom Stripe probably didn't tell the truth about the hiding place, but I feel confident he knows that Pierre Chap has been imprisoned somewhere."

The sheriff paid little heed to her words.

"Surely you aren't going to abandon the search for Mr Chap?" Nancy cried.

"Except for the ridiculous story Tom Stripe told you, what proof do you have that he has been kidnapped?"

"His house was boarded up, and I found a note in the oak tree."

"The message was probably put there for a joke. Go away and don't bother me," the sheriff said crossly.

Nancy tried to talk with some of the men and explain to them, but they did not seem to care to listen to her.

"Such an unreasonable lot," the girl complained later to Bess and George. "Instead of arresting Tom Stripe, they let him go free, and then blame me for it all!"

Norman Ranny was equally discouraged when he

returned to camp. He declared that he would set out alone and search for Pierre Chap.

"I thought when I sent for Annette that if she were to come here she might find her grandfather safe and well," Nancy told him. "Now, if she should arrive and learn that he is still missing, it may prove to be a great shock to her."

Since it was unlikely that the plane would return that evening, Nancy and her friends made plans to camp on the site. They had brought only the barest necessities with them, and spent an uncomfortable night. When morning dawned there was still no sign of the plane.

Mr Drew and his daughter were troubled at the delay. Buck Sawtice, on the other hand, did not seem the least bit disturbed. He kept his men busy removing gold from the surface vein.

"I don't like the way they're carting off the gold," Nancy complained. "After all, I haven't sold the land yet so they're really stealing from me."

"There's nothing we can do, I am afraid," her father told her. "The sheriff doesn't seem disposed to protect our interests here of late."

At noon one of the sheriff's men sighted a distant forest fire from the knoll. He reported it to his companions, all of whom prepared to ride away to fight it.

Except for Norman Ranny and his friends, the Dawsons, everyone had deserted the camp. Buck Sawtice could not conceal his pleasure as he watched the men ride away.

"They weren't really doing us any good," Mr Drew commented to Nancy when the two were alone, "although the psychological effect of their being here was worth while."

She nodded soberly.

"Now that the sheriff has gone, Buck Sawtice may try a few tricks."

"That's it exactly. I don't like the way he's acting."

"He seems entirely too confident about something. I can't understand why the plane hasn't returned with the money."

"Neither can I. It begins to look a trifle suspicious."

All that day the party waited. It was irritating to watch the miners at work, removing gold ore and nuggets which they chanced to find, but Nancy and her friends held their peace.

"If that plane doesn't arrive here by morning, I intend to have a showdown with Sawtice," Carson Drew told Ranny. "I'm beginning to think we've been tricked."

That night Nancy tossed restlessly in her blankets. Finally she dressed herself and left the tent.

It was a pleasant moonlight night. Everything was quiet about the camp.

"I'll take a short walk," Nancy decided. "Perhaps that will make me tired enough to want to sleep."

She had gone only a short distance through the trees when she saw the silhouettes of two men directly ahead of her. Creeping up closer, she heard them talking animatedly together in French.

"I'm sticking with Sawtice," she heard one of them say, "for he's a shrewd old fox. Why, I know for a fact that he never intends to pay Nancy Drew for this land. He told the pilot not to bring back any money."

"So!" the other chuckled. "In a few more days we'll have most of the nuggets from the creek. Nancy Drew and her father are like two blind cats—they see nothing!

And to think that Sawtice is locking the gold in a shack less than half a mile from here. Soon he will have enough, and then off we'll go to a richer field while they sit here patiently waiting for the money!"

The two men laughed heartily at the joke.

"It was a good joke the way they swallowed that story Tom Stripe told them about imprisoning Pierre Chap in the cave! The sheriff's men went riding all over the country, never suspecting that Chap was hidden almost within a stone's throw of the camp!"

The conversation ran on, finally changing to a less interesting subject. Convinced that she could learn no more, Nancy returned to her tent. The walk into the woods had certainly brought her no peace of mind. Until dawn the girl lay awake, thinking and planning.

Long before her friends were awake, Nancy was up and about. She hiked a short distance upstream, and came to a high dam, which she spent the greater part of an hour inspecting. Not far away there was a shack in which dynamite was kept. A sign warned all persons to keep away. Nancy surveyed the building with interest but did not try to enter it.

She returned to camp to find her father up and dressed, and immediately told him everything she had overheard. Bess and George came over to hear her story.

"I did a little exploring this morning," Nancy explained. "I thought I might find the shack where the gold nuggets are kept, but all I could see was a place where dynamite is stored."

"Why, I remember seeing an old shack not far from this camp," Bess said. "George and I were doing a little prospecting when we noticed the place. We would have investigated it, but Raymond Niles was around."

"Did he seem to be guarding the cabin?" Nancy questioned.

"Why, come to think of it, that might have been what he was doing. He looked relieved when we walked away, didn't he, George?"

"Yes, he did. Maybe he's keeping watch over the gold!"

"Can you point out the building?" Mr Drew asked the girls.

They assured him that they could do so.

"I have a feeling that Pierre Chap may be imprisoned near the gold shack," Nancy declared. "If we can locate the latter, we may be able to find him."

"Even if we should find the shack, it might not be easy to free Mr Chap," Carson Drew said thoughtfully. "We are greatly outnumbered by the miners."

"And they watch our every move," George added. "Bess and I can't stir a step from camp without being followed. Nancy is spied on too."

"I am disgusted with the way the sheriff failed us," Mr Drew commented. "I sent word for him to return, but I have no hope of his doing so."

"We can't afford to wait," Nancy said quietly.

"No. By delaying we will play directly into Buck Sawtice's hands. Yet I can think of no plan to outwit him."

Nancy leaned forward and lowered her voice.

"I have one," she announced.

## The Key to the Gold

BUCK SAWTICE was busily writing at a table in his tent when Nancy and her friends entered. He looked up sharply, then offered them camp chairs.

"Well, what is it?" he asked.

"I have come to see you about my land," Nancy began.

Before she could explain the proposition she had in mind, he cut her short.

"Now don't be alarmed because the plane hasn't returned with your money, Miss Drew. I feel certain the pilot will arrive today."

Nancy's eyes narrowed.

"You know as well as I do he'll never bring back the money, Mr Sawtice. You have tried to trick me."

The man's jaw dropped. He glanced quickly at Carson Drew, but the lawyer's grim expression told him more plainly than words that the truth had been discovered.

"Nonsense," he denied feebly. "I am as puzzled as you are over the delay, though I have every confidence that the pilot will not fail me."

"He will obey orders," Nancy retorted scornfully. "I happen to know that you told him *not* to bring the money. However, I am willing to make a new deal with you."

Buck Sawtice studied her shrewdly.

"You mean you'll take less for your land?"

"I'll give it to you for nothing—on one condition."

Carson Drew sprang from his chair.

"Nancy, do you realize what you are saying?"

"Absolutely," Nancy smiled.

"What is your condition?" Sawtice asked cautiously.

"That you return Pierre Chap unharmed!"

A mask-like expression froze upon the promoter's face.

"Who is Pierre Chap?"

"You know very well who he is," Nancy countered, "for he is hidden near this camp."

"You are mistaken, Miss Drew. I am not a kidnapper."

"I am making no accusations," Nancy retorted. "However, I feel confident that if you wish to do so you can locate Pierre Chap. Should you care to accept my proposition and have him safely in camp by nightfall, I will make my land over to the Yellow Dawn Mining Company."

"Nancy, you will lose everything by this deal," her father protested.

"I've thought it all over carefully, Father. If Mr Sawtice accepts the proposal, I intend to go through with it."

"Suppose I should return Pierre Chap—mind I don't say that I can—what proof have I that you will keep your agreement?" Sawtice demanded.

Nancy raised up her head proudly.

"You have my word."

"And do you agree to abide by this decision of your daughter?" the promoter asked Carson Drew.

"I suppose I must, though I'll admit it goes against the grain to do so."

"What do you say?" Nancy urged.

"If your father will sign the paper as your guardian, I'll agree."

"All right, I'll sign," Carson Drew snapped. "Now are you satisfied?"

"Quite," Sawtice smiled. "I really admire your daughter for her shrewd business ability, otherwise I would decline the proposal. You know, had I wished I could have taken the land without obligating myself in any way."

Carson Drew stifled a bitter retort as he escorted the girls to the door of the tent. When the four were out of earshot of Buck Sawtice they gave vent to their pent-up feelings.

"It was nothing less than stealing," Mr Drew declared angrily. "Nancy, I'd never have permitted you to go through with it, had I known what you proposed to do before we went into that tent."

"That's why I didn't tell you," the girl smiled. "I lay awake last night thinking and thinking. It seemed to me the only way to save Mr Chap."

"But you'll lose everything," George wailed. "They will get all the gold."

"According to Mr Ranny and the surveyor, the best part of it has already been taken from the land."

"But the gold really belonged to you," Bess maintained. "Buck Sawtice has no right to take anything until you deed the property to him. Isn't that correct, Mr Drew?"

"Yes, it is, Bess, but up here in the woods might seems to be right."

"I wish I could save the gold, though I don't see how I can," Nancy said regretfully. "After all, Pierre Chap's life is the most important consideration. You aren't really annoyed with me, are you, Dad?"

Her father squeezed her hand.

"No, I'm very proud of you, Nancy. You have been very generous. But it infuriates me to think that Sawtice is going to win out in this affair."

The lawyer dropped his voice as Sawtice emerged from his tent. They saw him walk across the field, and talk with several of his cronies, whereupon the four men rode out of the camp, leading an extra horse.

"They're going after Mr Chap," Nancy was confident. "Sawtice only pretended that he didn't know where to find him."

Carson Drew left the girls to talk with Norman Ranny.

"Now is our chance to get the gold," Nancy whispered to Bess and George. "I didn't dare mention all my plans when Father was here, for he wouldn't have allowed me to attempt it."

She then outlined what she proposed to do. Bess and George were frightened, but at her insistence they were willing to attempt to carry the plan through.

The girls quietly slipped away from camp. Bess, who remembered where the gold shack was located, led the way. A short distance from the hut they paused to talk over the situation.

"Raymond Niles is still there on guard," Bess observed.

"Then this is almost certain to be where the gold is kept," Nancy said with satisfaction. "Now, girls, don't forget your parts in our little play!"

Assuming an air of innocence, the three girls linked arms and strolled out into the clearing. Raymond Niles noticed them instantly, and watched them intently, but the girls pretended to be unaware of his scrutiny, and meandered towards him.

"Well, if it isn't Mr Niles!" Nancy greeted in surprise. "I was wondering where you had been keeping yourself lately. We haven't seen you in camp much."

Flattered to think that his absence had been noticed, the guard bestowed his best smile on the three.

"Is this your cabin?" Bess inquired politely.

"Well, not exactly. I sort of own a part interest in it. I look after it for another fellow."

"I'd love to see the inside," Nancy said wheedlingly.

"I wish I could let you, but it's impossible. The other fellow wouldn't like it."

"Oh," George sighed in pretended disappointment, "I did so want to peer inside. Of course, you don't mind if we just look in the window, do you?"

Before Niles was fully aware of her intention, she turned towards the window.

"Here, you mustn't do that," he cried, starting after the girl.

This was the opportunity Nancy sought. She had noticed that Niles held in his hand the key to the padlock on the door.

"Oh, please let us go inside," she pleaded, grasping him by the hand.

A foolish grin spread over the young man's face.

"I wish I could, Miss Drew, but I have to obey orders."

Nancy smiled as she quickly withdrew her hand from his. But she had the key in her possession!

"Oh come, on, girls," she called carelessly. "What do we want to see this silly old place for, anyway?"

Taking their cue, George and Bess followed her.

"Don't be in such a hurry," Niles begged. "Stay and talk a while."

They pretended not to hear him.

"Did you get the key, Nancy?" George demanded, when they were some distance away.

"I certainly did! Foolish fellow! He thinks every girl in the world is captivated by his charms."

"What do you intend to do with the key, now that you have it?" Bess inquired curiously. "If you're planning on getting that gold it won't be so easy."

"That's what I'm afraid of," Nancy admitted.

The day passed slowly. Towards nightfall men were seen coming slowly down the trail. They were leading another horse on which Pierre Chap was mounted. The old man was slumped in the saddle and nearly collapsed when Mr Drew and Norman Ranny hurried to help him. They half-carried him down to a nearby tent. Buck Sawtice did not give Nancy nor her father an opportunity to talk with Mr Chap.

"I've kept my part of the agreement," he told them. "Now you must do as you promised."

The girl had the deed ready. In rapid order, scarcely pausing to read them, she signed the papers which the promoter thrust into her hand. Almost sullenly, Carson Drew added his signature to the documents.

"There, the land is yours," he said bitterly, after the final sheet had been signed. "I presume it gives you intense satisfaction to cheat my daughter out of her property!"

Back in the tent where Norman Ranny was minister-

ing to the needs of Mr Chap, the Drews began to regret
having kept their agreement, for they were to learn
that the prisoner had been most inhumanely treated by
his captors.

"They beat me nearly every day," Mr Chap related
in a cracked voice. "They tried everything they could
think of to make me tell where I had hidden my
money. Even after Tom Stripe learned the truth, they
abused me shamefully."

"Did Buck Sawtice have anything to do with it?"
Nancy demanded.

"Yes, he was the ringleader. Everything was done
according to his orders. Even on the way here the men
beat me."

"It was included in the agreement that Mr Chap
should be returned unharmed," Nancy said bitterly.
"In every way Sawtice has broken his promises."

"If only you hadn't signed away the land!" George
groaned.

"It wouldn't have been necessary had we been
properly protected by the authorities," Carson Drew
snapped. "We are justified in taking the law into our
own hands."

"There should be some way of recovering stolen
gold," Ranny declared. "If you like, I'll march into
Sawtice's tent with my gun and demand a settlement."

"You would be overpowered in an instant," Nancy
said. "I think I have a better plan. I've already told
Bess and George about it. Wait here until we return."

The girls darted from the tent before they could be
stopped. Racing to the gold shack, they were delighted
to find that Niles had left his post.

Nancy unlocked the door. With George standing

guard, Nancy and Bess made a hasty search of the place. In one of the cupboards they found a heavy bag of gold nuggets.

"Quick! I think I hear someone coming!" George warned.

The girls grasped the precious gold, and ran as fast as they could back to the tent. She thrust the heavy container into the hand of her surprised father.

"Keep this for me! I have something more to do!"

As she was about to dash from the tent again, she paused to fling out some important instructions.

"Get Mr Chap out of here as quickly as you can. And everyone meet me in ten minutes at the place where our horses are tied!"

"What are you going to do?" Carson Drew called after her.

Intent only on her purpose, Nancy did not hear him. She ran up the path which led to the dynamite shack. It was her plan to change the course of the stream by blasting the power dam.

"It's a risky thing to attempt," she told herself grimly, "but if I succeed, Sawtice will never be able to use my property!"

# · 20 ·

## *Rushing Waters*

NANCY reached the shack, and was elated to find it unlocked. She carefully selected a large stick of dynamite from among the stores of explosive, and carried it gingerly to the dam.

Balancing herself dexterously, she moved far out on to the structure, and placed the charge so that it would explode in the most effective place. She hesitated an instant, and then struck a match, which she applied to the long fuse. The flame began to eat its way slowly towards the stick.

Pausing only long enough to make certain that the fire would not go out, Nancy turned and fled. She was out of breath when she reached her friends.

"Mount, and ride for your lives!" she gasped.

Carson Drew slung the heavy bag of gold over the saddle of his horse. Norman Ranny rode double, supporting Pierre Chap. They all raced for the knoll. Even before they reached it, they heard a terrific blast!

"What was that?" Mr Drew shouted, drawing rein.

"Don't stop now!" Nancy cried, striking at the flank of his horse. "Ride on! Ride on!"

They reached the hillock in safety. Then Nancy pointed with a trembling hand to the torrent of water that was flooding down the valley, and coursing over the ground they had recently left.

"You dynamited the dam!" her father exclaimed.

"Yes, for that was the only way I could prevent Sawtice from using my property. Now it will be covered with several feet of water. The mining tools and equipment will be destroyed, but I warned the workers to stay away from the valley."

Fascinated, the party stood on the high ground and watched the water as it spread out over the land. The camp had soon become a lake.

"I'm glad Sawtice and his men escaped," Nancy said soberly, "even though they are scoundrels."

Back in Wellington Lake, after Mr Chap's story had been told to the authorities, warrants were issued for the arrest of Buck Sawtice and his fellow conspirators. Tom Stripe and Raymond Niles were caught almost immediately, though several days passed before Sawtice was placed behind jail bars. He was to be tried for participation in many fraudulent schemes.

Shortly after, Annette Chap arrived by plane in response to the urgent message she had received. She had recovered rapidly from her accident, and looked almost as well as she had the day she first met Nancy.

"I'm not very strong yet," the writer confessed ruefully. "But I know I shall feel better after I've spent a few weeks here. Grandfather Pierre and I intend to get well together."

When Nancy saw the two of them, happy at being reunited, she never once regretted signing away her land. Of course, most of the valuable gold had been removed before the property was flooded. Yet had all the gold been lost, she would not have wanted things to turn out otherwise. Mrs Donnelly insisted that Norman Ranny remain at her home with the others, for due to

Nancy's efforts, there had been a reconciliation between the Ranny and Donnelly families.

In tracing the unscrupulous practices of the Yellow Dawn Company, it was proved that Tom Stripe had caused most of the trouble between the two women. He, too, had forged the document which had been received by the Velvet Company, and had sold a great many worthless shares. Both Mrs Donnelly and Mrs Ranny were overjoyed to learn that some of the money they had lost would eventually be returned to them.

"Speaking of money, I never dreamed that I was holding a small fortune in my hands when Nancy gave me that bag of gold," Mr Drew ruminated, as they were all seated before the crackling fire in Mrs Donnelly's sitting room. He chuckled softly to himself. "I guess it isn't the first time I've been left holding the bag!"

"How much do you suppose the gold will be worth?" Nancy queried.

"A very tidy sum," Norman Ranny told her. "Far more than your land would ever have brought you."

"I'll send it to the assayer's for you," Mr Drew promised. "How do you want it? In gold coins, or one huge bar?"

"I think gold coins would be more useful," Nancy said gaily.

Pierre Chap had looked highly distressed at the mention of money. When Nancy asked him what the trouble was he confessed to the group that his entire fortune had been stolen by Tom Stripe.

"I wanted Annette to have the money," he said sadly. "That scoundrel forced me to tell him where I had hidden the chest. Now, even though he has been caught, I doubt if I will ever get back any of it."

"Why, Mr Ranny and I dug up your chest and re-buried it," Nancy informed him. "Everything happened so rapidly that I completely forgot to mention it to you."

After a day of rest Nancy and her friends returned to the Chap cabin with the prospector, Annette and her grandfather. They found the chest where it had been hidden, not far from the ancient oak tree.

Before the girls returned to join Carson Drew at Wellington Lake where he was still busy gathering data concerning the Taylor lumber case, Annette Chap drew them aside for a little confession.

"Norman and I are to be married next week. We feel that we have waited too long as it is," she said.

"I am so glad," Nancy beamed. "I hope that I've perhaps had a tiny part in your happiness."

"You've been the whole cause of it," the novelist assured her gratefully. "As long as I live I shall never forget your kindness to me. Not only did you reunite Norman and myself, but you saved Grandfather's life."

"I think the hollow oak did it all," Nancy smiled. "If it hadn't been for the message left inside it, I can't imagine how things might have ended."

"Speaking of the hollow oak reminds me of another thing I have to tell you," the woman smiled. "Norman and I plan to build our new home on this very site."

"Near the oak tree?"

"Yes, for we've grown greatly attached to it. Besides, it's near Grandfather Pierre's cabin."

"Don't you feel sad to think of giving up your career as a writer and coming back home to live?" Nancy asked presently.

Annette shook her head.

"I'd gladly give it up, if need be. However, this is an ideal place in which to write. Although I shall have to stop my film work, there will be more time for me to write novels."

"I am sure you will be very happy here," Nancy said, smiling.

When Nancy and her friends returned to Lake Wellington they found that Carson Drew had completed all his business matters, and was eager to start back for the United States.

Before they left, the girls inquired about the condition of their former guide, Pete Atkins. Great was their relief to learn that he was well on the road to recovery.

"I wish you didn't need to hurry away," Mrs Donnelly protested, as she said goodbye to the girls.

"So do we," Bess and George told her in unison.

"We'll try to come back next summer, if you care to have us," Nancy declared. "But you must promise not to provide us with so much excitement."

Mrs Donnelly laughed heartily.

"I think the only way I could promise that would be for me to keep all of you locked up in one room!"

As they were en route to River Heights, Carson Drew disclosed that the trip north had been a highly successful one for him.

"I have absolute proof now that Buck Sawtice is involved in the Marcus Taylor lumber matter," he told the girls. "If I don't win that case now I'm not worth much as a lawyer."

When the train pulled into River Heights, Hannah Gruen rushed up to welcome the little group home.

"My! My! If it isn't good to have you home again," she cried. "It seems as if you've been gone a year."

Nancy smiled in appreciation. "I must admit it was one of the most exciting holidays of my life!"

At the time she did not realize that soon she was to become involved in an adventure just as thrilling, that of *The Invisible Intruder*.

"Did you bring the bag of gold with you?" the housekeeper whispered anxiously.

Nancy laughed gleefully.

"No, I'm thankful to say that Dad has relieved me of that responsibility. The gold is at the assayer's now. I won't know for several weeks how much I will receive for it."

Shortly after the Drews returned to River Heights, the Marcus Taylor case came up for trial. No one was surprised to learn that the lumberman had been awarded a large sum in damages, for Carson Drew had gathered such a vast amount of evidence that no other verdict would have been possible.

One day Nancy received a long letter from Annette Chap. The young woman enclosed a photograph of the famous old oak on the Chap property. Nancy put it away carefully in a drawer that held some of her dearest possessions.

The letter contained considerable news. Buck Sawtice had been brought to trial. He had been convicted on many counts, and sent to prison for a long term. Tom Stripe and Raymond Niles had escaped with lighter sentences.

After discussing the events Nancy sat on the arm of her father's chair, and playfully tweaked his ear. "As my legal adviser, how would you suggest that I spend my gold?" she asked.

Carson Drew thoughtfully blew several smoke rings

to the ceiling before answering. His eyes twinkled as he replied:

"I was just thinking that you might want to buy a little piece of land."

Nancy glanced ruefully at her father to see if he really was serious. Then she laughed heartily.

"Dad, if anyone should ever offer me another deed, I'd run a mile!" she said. "After having had so many exciting adventures up north, I think I'll agree to your holding title to all the property that comes into the Drew family!"